GW00587177

crisp

Crisp

r.w. gray

NeWest Press

copyright © r.w. gray 2010

— — —

Library and Archives Canada Cataloguing in Publication

Gray, R.W. (Robert William), 1969–
        Crisp [electronic resource] / R.W. Gray.

(Nunatak first fiction ; no. 29)
Short stories.
ISBN 978-1-897126-64-6
    I. Title.
    II. Series: Nunatak first fiction ; no. 29

PS8613.R389C75 2010   C813'.6   C2009-906234-8

— — —

Editor for the Board: Suzette Mayr
Cover and interior design: Natalie Olsen, Kisscut Design
Cover image: Nathalie Daoust, "Pilatus" (2007) from Frozen in Time, Switzerland, analog photography
Author photo: Christopher Smith

Excerpt from "Sonata with some pine trees" from EXTRAVAGARIA by Pablo Neruda, translated by Alastair Reid. Translation copyright © 1974 by Alastair Reid. Reprinted by permission of Farrar, Straus and Giroux, LLC.
    Every effort has been made to obtain permissions for all other excerpts. If there is an omission or error, the publisher would be grateful to be so informed.

NeWest Press acknowledges the support of the Canada Council for the Arts, the Alberta Foundation for the Arts, and the Edmonton Arts Council for our publishing program. We also acknowledge the financial support of the Government of Canada through the Book Publishing Industry Development Program (BPIDP).

NeWest Press

201. 8540–109 Street
Edmonton, Alberta T6G 1E6
780.432.9427
www.newestpress.com

1 2 3 4 5 13 12 11 10   printed and bound in Canada

For my brother Wayne and my mother Linda,
because we got through those early years together
and they know where all these stories come from.

contents

13 the bends

27 sweet tooth

37 waves

39 crisp

51 sunflowers

63 flamenco

65 wabi sabi

73 seeds

83 undertow

97 roughhousing

115 freighters

119 thirst

139 braille

141 the melancholy contortionist

157 acknowledgements

— — —

there are lands within the land
small uncared-for countries

"SONATA WITH SOME PINE TREES"
Pablo Neruda

He who lives more lives than one
More deaths than one must die

THE BALLAD OF READING GAOL
Oscar Wilde

Are you a beast of field and tree,
Or just a stronger child than me?

THE WIND
Robert Louis Stevenson

the bends

There's no way to tell the lifeguard that she is fine, that he need not have bothered to save her. Instead she thanks him profusely and says she must have eaten too much breakfast this morning, and that was what caused the cramps. He nods a lot, a smug saviour, and she aches to tell him that he is not what he thinks he is, but she just thanks him again and heads for the showers. Maybe he gets gold stars or medals for this kind of thing; she has no way of knowing. Maybe it makes him feel good, to save someone who appears so helpless. There are worse things than being convenient in someone else's life. Many worse things.

When Sarah steps out onto the street, it is already late afternoon and she finds the streets wet. The rain had been sudden, surprised the city, left it looking a little bruised. She wanders up the hill away from the bay, confused, looking for some answer, some explanation in the eyes of strangers in cafés. She is beside herself. She feels the birds begin to breathe again, and it seems to her that everyone is chattering, clacking words into the air, looking for one word, just one word to describe dust and moist at the same time. Is he still back there, underwater? She shouldn't be thinking about it. Ludicrous.

She stands in the square outside the pool, staring at the Saturday traffic crossing the Burrard Street bridge, the clouds rushing east off the water. It's late September, so the rain is seasonable yet still unexpected. There's so little you can control. Reading a magazine in the doctor's office, waiting for an appointment she'd forgotten and arrived half an hour late for, she had read a random fact: Earth is spinning on its axis at 1674.4 KM per hour, and hurtling around the sun at 108,000 KM per hour. She'd dropped the magazine onto the waiting room coffee table and rested her cold cheek against an upturned hand. Invisible speed depressed her deeply.

She remembers it now on the street, the hurtling and spinning, and she just wants to put her finger to her lips and say, "Shhhh," find some way to make the world suddenly quiet, suddenly still.

What if they could set aside five minutes when everyone in the world would just stand still, even grab hold of those damn butterflies and keep them still for a moment. What then? It wouldn't be that difficult. Half the world would probably be asleep anyway. But what then?

It's been three months and still Alice, Karen, and Tania take her to lunch once a week, setting aside a considerable portion of the meal to exercise their pity-pained faces, to hear the horror of what it must be like to be single at their age. They use words like "wounded" and "damaged," and remind her that she is "the victim." Some time is also devoted to tearing into Peter with suburban blood lust. They say Peter's heartless. He's arrogant. He's always flirted with them, even Tania, who admits she is less attractive than the other two because she wasn't born with blonde hair. They say he's always been emotionally stunted. He's nothing like their husbands.

Sarah imagines them arriving home after these lunches,

showering off her divorce bacteria and then applying ample moisturizer. Maybe they imagine Peter left her because she didn't have adequate ablutions. It's possible. Alice, Karen, and Tania never used to go for lunch with her. But they're her friends now. And this is what friends are for.

They say goodbye at the entrance to the restaurant, and they each slip her "care" packages. A "get slim" diet book from Tania (who hasn't cracked it open), some hand-me-down dresses from Alice, and from Karen just a business card, the number of her "wellness" coach. From this Sarah gathers that they and their reluctant husbands have chosen her over Peter. But she also deduces that they find her overweight, lacking style, and mentally unbalanced, and these are, in their minds, all potential reasons she couldn't keep the bastard in the first place.

Sarah remembers a ninth grade teacher telling her, "You're in for a rude awakening," though she doesn't remember why. Maybe this is it. This numbness. She's left her head somewhere. On the bus. At the corner store. In the pool.

She generally believes other people's stories before she believes her own, so these last few months have been overwhelming as she waits to feel "damaged," "wounded," or eventually "abandoned." What really scares her is that she doesn't feel anything. Their ex-relationship counsellor had said, "Feeling nothing is a mask for an abundance of feeling," and Sarah had wanted to point out that this must have been very reassuring for him and their hundred-dollar-an-hour sessions. Maybe it's not numbness, but just the fact that no one's fighting, no one's confused, and no one feels the overwhelming need to have the last word.

"Fine. See what happens," she says, grimacing hopefully when her friends ask her how she's holding up.

Her mother hasn't called in weeks. She might be giving Sarah some space, but it's more likely that this is dredging up "issues" from her own separation. She's probably taking "personal time" with her support group. Sarah's becoming certain that children spend their years until they're thirty trying to be different from their parents only to eventually sink, to creep back to what's sadly comfortable. It's in the lines forming in the corners of her eyes, in the dark, bruised shadows under them, in the fading colour of her hair, now more bland than blonde. It begins ever so subtly with a familiar gesture witnessed so often as a child. You start to throw salt over your shoulder when you spill a little, because that's what your father used to do. Then you begin to twist your hair around your finger the way your mother did when she was nervous.

"Are you all right?" asks a young man in a grey track suit. Sarah is startled, realizes she must have looked odd staring at the sky, standing in the middle of the square all this time. She looks at the young man and recognizes him as the life-guard from the pool; he must be finished his shift.

"I'm fine. The sky's just so beautiful," she replies, grabbing for a reason.

"Have a good night," he says as he walks away, looking over his shoulder twice to make sure she's not falling to the ground or drowning. A lifeguard's work is never done. For a moment Sarah wonders if he's flirting. Maybe it's not enough for him to save people at work. Maybe he wants to take her home and save her. She doesn't feel terribly averse to the idea. But she decides she's being foolish. People don't flirt with her. She doesn't know why. Maybe that's why her friends feel she won't make it without the asshole. He was the only one who ever saw fit to flirt with her.

She turns in the direction of home and starts to walk. Sometimes when it rains she takes the bus, but tonight she feels like walking. The lifeguard must think she's having a nervous breakdown, but she's quite happy. She has two cats, Eenie and Meany, but the first one lives up to the second's name. She goes to the gym each weekday evening and climbs and climbs on the machine made for climbing, stairs leading nowhere. She swims three times a week. Sometimes she looks in the mirror and imagines there must be someone, somewhere, who is pleased with her reflection, attracted to what she sees there, instead of this ... this remarkably arbitrary face. No, it's more than that. She's disquieted by the imitation of her face in the bathroom mirror, like bumping into someone familiar on a bus in a part of town where one would only encounter strangers. Familiar, yet wrong.

She's passing the markets along Davie Street when she hears a woman singing across the street.

"Why, oh why did you leave me?" She's a beautiful woman, maybe Korean, with a forlorn expression she's throwing out to traffic as it passes. Sarah is about to cross the street to hear the rest of the song, perhaps give the woman some money, when the woman turns and screams at the empty bus stop seat beside her. "Shut up! Just shut up!"

Sarah stops mid-stride and decides to stay on her side of the street. She turns to the nearest shop window and pretends to look at the display. It's a bakery, so she tries to justify buying cookies. She doesn't often eat cookies, but maybe just a small package of oatmeal ones to dip in tea. Then she sees, on the lowest shelf in the bakery's glass window, those small chocolate cookies she used to eat as a child; they were her favourite. Was it her father or her mother who baked them? She can't remember. Nothing worse than vague nostalgia. It's not like her, not at all, but she almost cries right there, just outside the window.

She enters, asks for the cookies with contained excitement, and finds herself wanting to explain her nostalgia to the baker. She's afraid of how often she now feels the urge to reach out to strangers, and each time it happens she remembers being a child, then a teenager, shopping with her mother. She remembers watching her mother talk to complete strangers, tell them how Uncle Howard's lost all the hair on his body, how her older sister's acne was probably related to diet, and various other details of her life, of their family's life. She's certain this led to her own shyness, her fear of divulging too much. The therapist had said this was her issue. Reticence. Was it loneliness that made her mother talk to strangers? Maybe this is what turns old women crazy and leads them to rant on buses about their lack of teeth and the voices inside their heads—maybe they just need to share with strangers, to reach out past the loneliness.

Suddenly Sarah's crying—a sob escapes her mouth and her hand jumps to catch it, but too late.

"Are you okay?" the man behind the counter asks, concern crinkling his forehead.

She digs into her purse, grabs a bill, and places it on the counter. The audacity of strangers. Is she okay? What kind of question is that? It's probably a bloody come on, or even worse, some pitiful way to make himself happy, benevolent in the face of the boredom of his own dreary existence. She doesn't really believe that. Working with cookies, with *these* cookies, couldn't be dreary. Couldn't.

"I'm fine. Thank you," she says as curtly as possible.

She waves away the plastic bag, nestling the paper bag
of cookies in her open purse. She turns and exits, the
bells above the door echoing, the cold air on her face,
the sidewalk thick with strangers. She forgot her change
but she's not going back. She notices her purse is still open
as a wide, square-jawed man walks into her, knocking her
to the ground, her purse exploding across the concrete
into a galaxy of lost details. He doesn't stop. No one stops.
Though they do watch her move slowly to collect her
lipstick, her daybook, the cookies. Her palms burn and
her knee is throbbing where it hit the sidewalk.

Sarah stands, her purse lighter. She didn't collect everything. She thinks of the cookies and decides she got what
she needed.

"Why oh why ... oh why?" wails the crazy woman on
the other side of the street, her sing-song lament outside
the supermarket. Then, with perfect timing, she turns
to her imaginary companion and yells, "Shut up! No one
asked you!" She grimaces. She looks up to the sky, her face
softens, her hands release with what looks like reverence
for the sky. Then suddenly her hands and her face clench
again, and she weeps, "How could you, oh why?"

Sarah rubs her burning palms against her skirt, then
brushes a wet strand of hair back off her forehead. Sure
it's hard, with no one to confide in. No one to ask about
things. No one to call out from other rooms. She needs to
relax. Maybe go for a massage or take a yoga class. Karen
mentioned yoga. No, that was Tania. Karen mentioned
her happy coach. Yoga, that's what she'll do. Something
to get her back into her body, so maybe then she won't be
so absentminded. She starts up the street to her apartment,
looking into the faces of strangers, wondering if she'd

recognize him. Then she feels foolish and focuses on her footsteps, the rain on her forehead, not looking anymore.

Absentmindedness led her into trouble back at the pool. She'd slipped into the area where people usually swim careful, corded-off laps. She was so preoccupied with thoughts of the conversation she'd just had with Peter over coffee that she didn't hear the lifeguard's calls. She began her lengths and didn't realize something was wrong until she was already above them in the deep end of the pool. At first she only thought it was peculiar that there were streams of bubbles erupting from below, tickling around her. Then she noticed where the bubbles came from. She didn't know what to do at first, just stopped mid-stroke and did what her third grade swimming instructor called the dead man's float. She didn't want to leave the streams of bubbles.

It's late, well past midnight, and she is now standing at the living room window looking out at the city lights, the strange Christmas tree effect of other people's lives flickering just out there. She turns to the dining table where she discarded her purse, digs and finds the cookies. There are a few left. He wants her back. She hasn't told any of their friends, her friends. He came to her two weeks after she'd moved out, told her he was regretful, three kinds of sorry, and wanted them to start anew. He used that word: anew. Rhymes with "poo," she thought to herself, and then tried not to laugh. Peter would think she was going crazy. He said he didn't want a response, but that's the sort of thing people say when they want you to say yes right now or later but not no. He said he wanted her to think about it. She had wanted to laugh, not just about the poo rhyme. It was a laughable moment. But she couldn't even let herself smile. She excused herself and went to the washroom. It would have probably crushed the man to see her smile right then, and she didn't want to crush him. She didn't want to hurt him in any way. In the washroom she looked in the bathroom mirror, hoping someone, even just her own reflection, might tell her what to say or do.

Back at the table, she sat across from him, looked out the café window, tried to focus on the lights of traffic glistening off the wet street, the hiss of passing cars so she wouldn't ask, "What about her?" And then she asked. She hated herself before the pronoun was even out of her mouth. She knew Peter could give her no honest answer.

He told her then how he had only had the affair with that woman because he was scared. That woman, she thought to herself. That woman. It sounded so powerful. He used words like "co-dependent" and phrases like "cognitive error," and she began to regret ever suggesting they seek couples counselling. It's much easier to give a monkey a hammer than it is to take it away.

That was four months ago, and since then they've tried to be friends: coffee "dates," movies he seemed to have carefully chosen for their messages about relationships, and walks where they carefully avoided the lagoon or the rhododendron park where they had discussed the end of their relationship. All the while, Peter waits for his yes.

Her mother seems to wait for it, too. She calls after each date and tries to sound casual as she asks how it went. Maybe Sarah wants the yes, too. Maybe. There's only one thing she knows for sure. Only after the numbness goes away will she know what to do.

At the pool today, her casual mistake. She floated motionless, just under the surface of the water, the streams of bubbles tickling past her to the surface. On the bottom she could count eight scuba divers, and she could see one of them sitting on the bottom looking up at her. He didn't gesture to any of his scuba friends, seemed separate and away from the others and their scuba language, carrying on with their scuba lives. He just sat on the bottom looking right at her as his breath ascended and fizzed around her to the surface. Effervescence, bubbles of his breath, warm and salty, turning her to breath, joining his. So she laughed. She read somewhere that castaway sailors surrounded by dolphins trying to save them could drown laughing, the sonar tickling their diaphragms, leaving them tragically breathless. Plenty worse ways to die.

She has always been very good at holding her breath. In the pool, she had remembered watching a television special on yogis who could hold their breaths and slow their heart rates until they were almost dead. She wondered, once they started, how did they stop themselves? She thinks this might happen to her. When she's reading or editing at work she forgets to breathe. Her assistant asks her why she sighs the way she does, but she needs to take a big breath like that when she's forgotten to breathe for a while.

She finds herself holding her breath when she's around Peter, too. When they see a movie or go for coffee, he will always talk about how much he's changed, and she has to consciously remind herself to breathe and unclench her hands. Yesterday when they chatted, he was going on about "family models" and his childhood, what he now saw as the source of all his relationship "rackets." Like most of the converted, it only took a few sentences before he suggested she try on his religion.

"Have you looked at your family background? Don't take this the wrong way, Sarah, but it might be telling, how no one in your family gets along." That had been the end of that coffee date. She didn't let him know he'd pissed her off, just found a quick and economical way to get out of there — something about the cats and an incident with a raccoon.

She'd always thought Peter had the most wonderful upbringing. It was one of the first things he told her about himself. How he had been the blonde-haired, blue-eyed, robust chosen one, and his parents seemed to have supported him through everything. Now that he had revised that whole story and found the roots of his issues (controlling mother, spineless father), she became suspicious of his stories. Arriving home after that bad date, she had turned on the light in the hallway in the middle of realizing she had spent the whole evening and the trip home thinking about Peter's revised history.

Maybe it isn't only his fault his stories take up so much space. After he left her for that woman, she felt relief, that maybe now she could stop thinking about him so much, might have time to look into her own story, wonder about her upbringing, maybe even discover some repressed memories. Anything. She went in search for this when she left Peter, but his stories, with their coffee dates, re-emerged, rewritten, bigger than ever. She realized then, standing in the hallway with her jacket still on, that Peter would never cease to find himself interesting. That once he had excavated this new version of his childhood, he would find another. How does he not drown in so many stories?

She goes to bed at 1:00 AM, knowing full well that she'll be awake for two or more hours, but she is determined to find sleep. When she closes her eyes, she's descending through the bubbles, floating down to the man sitting on the bottom of the pool, enclosed in that thick underwater silence she loves so much. Why is it that, on the surface, pools are so chaotic, so noisy, full of the sounds of children's voices echoing off tile walls? It's why she could not hear the lifeguard's whistle, did not notice the life preserver he threw in her vicinity. It's why she was startled by the crashing splash, flurry of limbs, rush of voices calling through water as he jumped in to save her, hooking his arm around her arm and across her chest, pulling her up and back so she surfaced. She got only one last glimpse of the scuba diver before the cloud of bubbles obscured her view. Then she was breaking the surface and a young man was telling her she was "going to be all right. Just breathe!" His strong left arm crushed her against his warm chest, and pulled her back and towards the edge of the pool. She rapidly blinked her eyes—the chlorine, the glare of the fluorescent lights, the shrieks of playing children. She realized she was crying.

Being saved wasn't wholly unpleasant. It was like being held. Like being safe, just for a moment. But then she was jostled free of the water, lifted and dropped on the cold, slick tiles, the lifeguard's warm arms gone. The whole incident might have been embarrassing to some, and even to Sarah, but any chance of embarrassment was buried under the pain of being tugged away from the deeper water, the cloud of bubbles, and the scuba diver's upturned face. She could live with the fact that she is probably a story the lifeguard will later tell someone, maybe a girl he wants to impress who wouldn't notice him otherwise, the kind of girl who counts brushstrokes as she combs her hair at night. Sarah could live with that. If only she could know that she is a story the scuba diver will tell someone—anyone.

The next morning she goes through her rituals, follows the script. The same breakfast, the same chewing, the same shower and soap and then clothes from the same closet. There is no story here, she thinks. She's not sure where she will find it.

At the bus stop she stands in the rain waiting for the bus to take her to work. Her hair tendrils down her forehead. It's early before the rush, and she's the only one there. She idly wonders where the crazy lady goes at night. Maybe home to her husband and kids, making macaroni like nobody's business, asking them about their days and never letting on that she sings and screams her afternoons away downtown among the strangers. Sarah looks down at the empty bench and then, before she can think, she's looking at the empty seat beside her. She's a little disappointed. She doesn't feel like singing. She doesn't feel like yelling at the empty seat. She considers trying anyway, wonders if she'll feel differently once she gets the ball rolling. Instead, she reaches out her hand and places it gently on the blank bench beside her. There's a beginning. She can sense it now. But it's still a long way under.

sweet tooth

i

4 ripe avocados, pitted and peeled
6 tablespoons fresh lemon juice
3 cups low-fat, plain yogurt
4 large fresh basil leaves, slivered
¼ teaspoon freshly ground pepper
4 large fresh basil leaves, for garnish
4 radishes, finely chopped, for garnish
Pinch of salt

They served a cold soup first, and it seemed like a perfect choice for such a warm evening in early June. The soup had almost been an afterthought, for the rice required so much attention that the soup, and most of the meal, became insignificant. Everyone had tasted the rice, a wild breed, and the general consensus was that it was not yet cooked, so more water was added and it was cooked some more, and then more water and more cooking. Wild rice is the most difficult to cook; the grain never reaches the texture one would expect. Eventually, hunger caused the guests to call the rice cooked and sit at the table, at first without the cold soup.

August's grandmother used to tell her that on particularly hot days one should drink hot tea to cool down. That if one drinks cold liquids, the body thinks it is cold and acclimatizes itself accordingly. So it follows that although the cold soup was refreshing in the heat of an early summer evening, it may have only increased the fervour of those who consumed it. And who would have thought, passion and cold soup.

ii

2 small Italian eggplants, cut into one-inch cubes
1 pound very new potatoes
  (the kind you can easily hold in the palm of your hand)
4 tablespoons olive oil
1 green and
1 red bell pepper, both cored, seeded, and cut into one-inch squares
1 red onion, coarsely chopped
6 ripe plum tomatoes, cubed
2 cloves garlic, minced
Salt and pepper to taste
A handful each of the following: parsley, basil, and oregano

They each tell stories of their childhood. Jamie confesses to making a neighbour boy drink a mix of juice crystals and his own urine. August admits she used to eat things she found on sidewalks, though, as Jamie points out, a hostess should never make such confessions. But it is Robert who tells a story from Tim's childhood. He talks of a young boy without a father. At night, after a long day on the canning lines, his mother must bathe each of his brothers and sisters before putting them to sleep. Only after bathing all four children would she draw herself a bath. The boy remembers lying in a tucked-in bed and hearing the sound of rushing water, and this sound becomes for him another word for sleep. Even now, as an adult, the sound of rushing water subdues him and fills him with fatigue. A school trip to Niagara Falls was almost fatal.

Tim blushes, tries to pretend the story hasn't been told, intends to wipe his mouth, but can't find his napkin. A polite smile, he looks out the window.

Thinking about water falling, Robert takes Tim's hand under the table. Then he stands and goes to the kitchen to refill the water jug. There, with the jug in his hand and the water beginning to flow cold from the kitchen tap, Robert thinks of the story he has just told. Once when Tim had a terrible flu, Robert left the water running in their tiny bathroom, wishing he could amplify the sound, longing to ease Tim to sleep. They have been together four times and broken up three, met so many times that they've been able to let go of all the faces that could have kept them apart. But now Tim is moving, to the other coast. And Robert is staying. Irreducible facts.

iii

The last bite of food bitten, the cutlery akimbo on empty plates, August gives Jamie a small smile as the heat swells in and replaces the conversation. Outside the windows, the cicadas dirge in the swelter, and in the kitchen, water rushes through the taps as Robert fills the water jug. Tim stifles a yawn brought on by the sound of rushing water, then blushes.

Jamie wonders if Robert has always been this way, how he fills a room. Robert is the type of man who tells stories, while Tim, Jamie notices, is the kind of man stories are told about. Jamie wonders if it's a trick of physiology suggested by Tim's plump mouth and thick neck. Or maybe because he talks less. Even now, as Tim shyly looks down at his own solid tradesman hands, he leaves much to the imagination. When he brings his glass to his mouth, there is something unconscious and deliberate. A closer look would show how his tongue reaches out to touch the glass, as though he trusts it more than his bottom lip to ensure the rim is there. Robert turns and sees August looking at Tim, too. His mouth, Jamie thinks.

"What were you like as a child?" Tim asks Jamie. August smiles and looks at her husband.

"Smaller, but the same size head," says Jamie.
August and Tim try to think about Robert as a child, how he seems to have come into the world as an adult with no history, no memories, no photos of himself naked at two, sitting in a creek bed. Each of them marvels at how they could love the man without noticing the missing past.

The casserole, too, is a secret recipe, and Jamie hasn't ever given out the ingredients without forgetting to mention something. Maybe a tablespoon of lemon zest, grated.

iv

And when the meal is mostly finished, August begins to clear the table, walking from the kitchen to the dining room and back again, making as many trips as possible to avoid either room. In the kitchen, her husband Jamie feeds the dog, while in the dining room her past love Robert laughs and tells a story to the one he loves now, Tim. She can still remember the V of his chest hanging over her, the smooth length of his back under her hands. Jamie's back is hairy.

Hands balancing dishes, she glances at Robert, his head tilted down to look at Tim's hands in his.

She passes Jamie who returns to the table. In the kitchen she wonders if Robert fantasized about a man like Tim when they were together; she remembers the small apartment they shared in Winnipeg, the one with too many doors for its two rooms and the late night scrapes and shouts of ice skaters on the frozen, flooded tennis courts out back. She doubts he remembers.

Stacking dishes next to the sink, she idly tastes a piece of chicken off Jamie's plate. She remembers making the meal, the list of ingredients, she remembers even tasting it to be sure she hadn't forgotten anything. She'd put a little too much garlic in the eggplant, but not enough salt. But she doesn't remember the taste of the meal as they sat at the table. Someone, maybe Tim, had complimented her and she'd nodded. But she couldn't remember any flavours between the making of the meal and this moment, closing parenthesis over dirty dishes. An argument for eating alone, without the distraction of other people, she thinks, eating another bite from Jamie's plate.

With a deep breath she returns to the table, poises on the edge of her chair, hoping she might find glasses or side plates that still need to be cleared. Jamie's hand rests on her hip and so she looks at him, a reflex. A tender smile. He has a spot of cold soup in the corner of his mouth. She reaches to her feet to find her napkin, expecting it's dropped, but can't find it.

"The corner of your mouth," she says, sticking her tongue out to show him how to reach the spot of soup.

He sticks his tongue out the opposite direction.

"Got it?" he asks.

"Yes," she says, and looks away from the spot of soup.

ʋ

It was a dinner punctuated by the hot summer wind rustling the window blinds and the dog running off with the table napkins. Jamie finds her in the kitchen, looking out at the small yard behind the house. The first thing they did when they moved into this house was tear up the bricks and plant grass so the dog could play in the five-by-twelve space. A snapshot of a life, but who knew if the dog cared?

Jamie wonders what August is thinking, and where she has been with those blue eyes. She cut her index finger while slicing red peppers for dinner, and just the sight of the Band-Aid hurts him. Her family are prone to fainting, and she had to sit on the floor with the half pepper in her hand, crushing its waxy texture. In pain she is unreachable, but this distraction of hers, at least, is familiar to him.

He returns to the table, to their guests, and August returns, perching on her chair and surveying the table. She is away and gone. He touches her on the hip with his open palm, cupping her warmth and softly bringing her attention around. He has learned to economize his touch, to express the most affection in the smallest gesture.

How he came so far in this life to this house, this home, this wife with the red pepper—it seems a mystery to him now. In the other room is his friend, his wife's past lover, and the lover's current lover. This dinner's guests.

And this is how it is meant to go. Three years of marriage culminate in a dinner party where the food doesn't satiate the appetite, and the light flush of the wine masks sensual stirring. He knows three languages, yet would he confess in any of them the way he finds himself looking at this young man, Tim, at this dinner party tonight? Perhaps not a kind of thirst, but only an undercurrent on this strange beach.

Something he will never let carry him away, but still … there is this strange sensation of colder water pulling on his feet. Another world, a few feet down.

This young man is the geography of a place he will never visit, only lines on a map he traces lightly with his finger. These subtle loves, these subtle passions are harmless when one is married. The next morning he can blame it on the wine … a brash and crass Argentinean grape, incidentally, though the guests liked it.

The kettle calls from the kitchen and his wife walks from the room with a consoling smile. Even a stranger could see she is a dancer. A ballet dancer, since it must be known that dancers of different styles walk differently. Modern dancers pound the earth with their feet, expecting an answer in return. But this woman, a ballet dancer, seems always, always about to rise up through the ceiling on an unexpected current, limbs like jellyfish tendrils, to suddenly disappear one Sunday afternoon so quietly even the dog would not start barking.

And then what? What would this man, her husband, do then? He can't float away. Not in this body at least, corduroy and belly flesh. It's a body that has worn him well, but some days, lately, it feels like laundry day underwear, the saddest, most shameful pair. He's still in very good shape, but after each run the small of his back clenches and whines. More often than not, he wants to stay home on weekends with the dog and the comfort of knowing August will soon be there with something chocolate from the local pâtisserie. She loves him in a Hansel and Gretel way.

Growing older with half-imagined passions and a sweet tooth. The crème brûlée. The forgotten dessert. He moves to the fridge, removes the small ceramic dishes full of cream (he jokingly calls them pudding for adults) and follows his wife into the dining room. For the briefest moment as the kitchen door swings open, he catches sight of Tim and Robert holding hands across the table, before they turn to greet him or the dessert.

vi

Robert watches first August, then Jamie enter the room from the kitchen. He remembers reading somewhere that if both of your hosts are in the kitchen for more than three minutes, all is not well. But despite the small dimple that has formed between August's eyebrows, there is no evidence of a disagreement on Jamie's face.

In the middle of a joke, and to punctuate his description of the jarring his sister's car caused the house when she drove into it, Robert bumps the hanging lamp above the dining room table with his palm. For the rest of the evening the light will continue to sway, as though on a ship on open waters.

Laughter ricochets between wine glasses, followed by a silence in which they each think of sleep and wonder if the evening has not gone on too long. Tim takes Robert's hand underneath the table and August wipes adult pudding from the corner of Jamie's mouth with her thumb.

vii

2 cups fresh cream
4 separated egg yolks
½ cup sugar
1 tablespoon real vanilla
1 cup brown sugar

The taste of the crème brûlée is indescribable. One man would call it "better than sex," another would say "a pleasure unlike any other," and yet another would only smile and say that "time is measured more carefully, more painfully with a good dessert." And you see, the woman said nothing. For it was painful enough for her to hear the men diminish such pleasure. With each spoonful she languished, tasted each mouthful as though alone in the room.

The final scraping of the small, white ceramic bowls signals an end to this dinner. Two men will leave and one will stay. The woman and the man will leave the dishes soaking in the sink and will fall asleep, each to their own side of the bed.

The dog sleeps in the kitchen tonight, dreaming, the taunting smell of dinner's dishes piled high in the sink.

waves

I've never slept with a whale trainer before. It makes me trust you. The way you must love something so much bigger than yourself.

Do you miss her? No, that's not what I was going to ask. I was thinking about her floating under the water, as broad and heavy as six city buses. In the quiet. Yeah, I guess it's probably not all that quiet. I wasn't imagining the screaming kids. I guess what I was wondering is if she thinks of you, these thick hands, wonders where you are.

Her, weightless and caught. They say dolphins cornered in a pen won't leap free: they can't imagine the other side. Yet she must know there's a world outside of the screaming kids and the lapping water, and must know you're there now, with another whale or another trainer. A less watery place where she can't follow.

A crusty and scraped history of her body, barnacle loved and net lashed. And me, no different from her, what you read smooth along my thigh, plain across my sacrum, erratic and gulping in the small white marks where I grew too fast one summer, and too in the stern line of an appendix scar from the year I left home. Subtler marks, too, here under my ribs and on the closed-fist pulse of my flung-back neck.

They say a grown man can stand and walk through the chambers of a grey whale's heart.

When I was fourteen, I paper-bagged groceries in a corner store. A man like you came in every Monday to buy groceries. Salt scent of fish guts and glitter scales crusted to wooden docks. He wore big gum boots. The cashier, she thought he was a fisherman, just like her ex-boyfriend. But I knew. Saw it in the way his eyes crinkled in the corners fanning to block the fluorescent lights, and in the thickness of his grizzled hands, confused, fidgeting. The beached slump of his shoulders, relieved to be free of the gull cries and nudging waltz of the docks, but holding his breath between his teeth. The way you grip your breath now, like you might lose it. I knew he too had a whale. A whale's song echoes clarion across leagues, through seaweed languishing, through furtive schools, through bare skin.

The air so thin between our lips, sheen of the wet wrung out of you, she floats closer. How long until she thinks you won't return? Always drifting towards you, as you look up at the hovering gulls, the profile of an oblivious man bleached by the sun. Just like you lie here pretending you're sleeping, and I lie beside you pretending that this is the happenstance. The sleeping man in my bed who smells faintly of fish. That this wasn't what I was looking for. How you'll leave in the morning and how I'll pretend that all I hear is the quiet water as I drift.

Crisp

It's Tuesday and our father has packed the trunk of his rusty blue car. I am seven, my brother Randy is five, and we're both standing on the porch. What neither of us says out loud is that we're relieved. We watch him load the last of his stuff into the car. The lamp with the tassels from the living room and his dining room chair, the one with the arms. Now there will be only three chairs left. I think to myself that the lamp and the chair are signs he isn't coming back. He's taking everything he could need. Then I see a storm in the south bunching up where the highway and the horizon meet, and I worry this is a sign he's going to stay. I tetherball back and forth this way.

Randy stands and stares. He grips a rock in his right hand and I wonder if he's going to throw it. I say nothing to him. I'm not a very good older brother. Mom pushes the screen door open and stands between us. Her left hand is over her mouth, her right hand props her elbow to keep her mouth in place. I can hear the thunder now. I want to call to Father as he opens the door, say maybe he should wait out the storm. But he nods before I can and gets in.

The car shudders, a plume of blue smoke erupting towards us on the steps. He doesn't wait for it to warm up, just backs up, then the car moves forward and away. His left arm reaches out the window and waves a slow wave.

Thunder again, and I look up to the rain suddenly falling on my face, the storm here already, like it just remembered it should rain and is making up for lost time. She starts to cry then, our mom. Maybe she thinks the rain will hide her tears, the telltale red of her run-ragged eyes. Or maybe she doesn't care.

We watch him drive the half mile to the end of the driveway, driving into the storm, the clouds mud grey and the lightning cracking in the big sky. His car stops at the highway. He doesn't signal. The car idles, long enough for me to think maybe he'll turn around and come back. Maybe he's thinking about Randy and me. How we need a father. One one thousand. Two one thousand. What's he waiting for?

A bolt of lightning rips through the air above the highway, smites Father's rust-pocked blue car, and it explodes as the gas tank turns electric. Mother's hand flies off her mouth and she lets out a strange animal shriek; she starts to laugh, everything tumbling out of her mouth at once. She had been nagging him for weeks to get the gas tank fixed. It was leaking gas everywhere. The back seats, the carpet—they were wet with it. So it could have been the car cigarette lighter that pops clear of the dash when ember hot. But I prefer to think it was the lightning, that God has something to do with it. Because only God can smite things.

Mom's face clinches red and raw in the rain, the laughter spilling out of her a little angry then a little sad then a little angry, and on and on. I see Randy look down. Yellow liquid runs down Mom's legs from her short denim shorts. She's peeing herself, a yellow puddle forming around her bare feet on the deck. The rain's falling harder now, splashing the urine. Randy looks like he's going to say something, but I give him a full-force look. I give him the look that he and

I both understand means just look at the horizon, look at the smouldering metal of our father. We are rocks, Randy, just look at the horizon.

What if he's still alive? I take a step forward, a lurch.

"He's dead," says Randy. "He's burnt to a crisp now."

But my feet are staggering forward, I start to run, my bare feet numbly hitting sharp gravel on the muddy driveway, and I am running the long distance to the highway, to the burning wreckage. I run to see for myself. And I run partly to get away from the word *crisp*.

Randy is smaller than me but he can outrun anyone. Halfway to the highway, halfway to the burning metal skeleton, he tackles me to the ground. My palms burn from the gravel but the mud soothes them. He doesn't say anything. I know he's right. There's nothing to see in the car. Miles away, in town, we can hear the fire engine's siren. They must have seen the explosion.

The firefighters arrive in a flurry of trucks and hoses and yellow hats. They stand around and talk about what to do, whether the rain's got it covered or not. They tell us to go back to the house. They call a tow truck, but the car won't stop burning. They stride to the porch where Mom stands. The rain has washed away the urine. They must think she's just wet from the rain and the tears.

"It doesn't look good," says one firefighter. The others nod. They think it's the rubber in the tires that keeps the car burning. They don't really know.

Randy glares at them. I see he's still holding the rock.

Our mom has a strange love for rocks. She talks about it sometimes, where she thinks she got that love. That summer when she was seventeen and her little sister was fifteen, the same distance apart as Randy and me. That summer they

drove all over the place in my mom's Volkswagen Bug.
It was an old one, the kind with the running boards, and
the last owner had broken the mechanisms for both the
windows, so everywhere they went that summer they baked
in that car and had to drink tons of water, but they never
had to pee as they just sweated it all out. Mom always said
that part like she was offering a handy tip.

The one time, they were driving up some dirt road thinking they might find some swimming hole where they could
go skinny dipping. The road they drove on was strange,
though, and the sides of the road started to rise and the
road itself began to narrow. Her sister thought they should
turn back, but Mom decided they should keep going. Rocks
scraped against the undercarriage, and the trees crowded
in closer, branches dragging along the windows.

With a grinding shudder, the car lurched to a stop. My
mother's sister turned and looked out the back window and
could see where they'd gone, could see that this wasn't a
road after all. The stones were too rough, the shapes not flat
enough. This was a riverbed. A dry riverbed. The stones on
the side had narrowed until the car was wedged and could
go no further.

They had to back up for miles. They backed into the first
side road and found themselves beside a burnt bridge and
a real river. My aunt pulled the latch but her door wouldn't
open. My mother tried, too. Hers wouldn't budge either.

"I told her to throw her shoulder into it," my mother said.
"But from that all's we got were two bruised shoulders, one
apiece."

In a flash she wondered if they would die in that car.
They honked the horn and yelled and screamed through the
stuck windows. They had a little water left, a few mouthfuls.

Then there he was. A river god of a man, all curly hair and cut-off shorts. He smiled at them.

He pointed to the bottom of my mother's car door, laughed and hollered through the glass, "Your running boards are all bent up."

My mother shrugged, a playful shrug, a what-can-you-do shrug, giving him plenty of room to be their saviour.

He found a big enough rock and broke her driver's side window, using his shirt to pull out the few shards of glass still caught in the door so the two sisters could climb out. They swam together that whole day in the sun, and he taught her to skip rocks across the slow, lanky river. At the end of the day, the sisters climbed back in that driver's side window and drove away, waving to the river god.

When she tells this story I sometimes ask about him, see if I can get her to describe him more. I think he's the most beautiful man in the world. But I also have this feeling in my stomach like slipping in the tub as I see the look in her eyes, like she wants to be somewhere else. Like she wants to go back there. It's my favourite Mom story because she squints funny when she tells it, like she's closer to it for squinting. And in her eyes, you can see she is closer.

She collects flat rocks wherever we go. But there's no place to skip them here. The lakes are far off. And the gullies too small.

A few days later, one of the firefighters comes back. He says he's come to check on our father's burning car. And then later another. And then other men. In the days after Dad exploded, many men come around. The ones who nod before they close her bedroom door and the ones who don't look at me after they ask, "Is your mother home?"

Randy and I sit in the kitchen and eat cereal. I ask him

if he thinks it's weird that there are so many firemen in our town.

He shrugs his shoulders. "Maybe we have a lot of accidents." He's acting sullen.

There's a knock on the screen door. It's another firefighter. "Is your mother home?"

Randy slumps over further in his chair. The man walks down the hall to our mother's room. Her moans begin again. My little brother Randy watches a lot of nature shows. He says animals communicate through noise, that a baby's cry can make a mother's breasts leak milk. I ask him what about a mother's cry, but he says he hasn't seen anything about that. "I gotta go someplace," says Randy, and he's out the door.

I'm not a very good older brother to Randy. I mostly read superhero comics and lay in my bed. I don't play ball with him, never learned to spit without spraying everywhere, and he's always been the one who protects me. I watch out the windows as Randy orbits, throwing rocks so they nick the boards that hide the trailer wheels. He does this every time a man comes over now.

I learn to cook. I cook all the time. I mean I learn to cook, not just heat up things from cans. Because we can't just eat cereal and because I have to be some kind of older brother to Randy. I learn to cook with raucous, banging pans and slamming cupboards, all the while singing songs that don't exist. Randy comes back for the food, but also because he can't hear Mom's moans over all my noise. This is how I will be an older brother.

Mom doesn't come out of her room except to pee, and then she sometimes walks the length of the trailer and stands in the door to the kitchen in her thin nightie, her breasts and other stuff filling up the trailer. She smells of

Old Spice and the ocean. It's a small trailer. We live pressed in on one another this way. My brother and I both nod. And then she says, "Cook yourselves something to eat. I have to sleep." She shuffles down the hall and back to her bedroom.

Then the men stop coming around as much, though a few still come back again and again. There's this one, a potbelly like it's full of worms, a cartoon red nose, and Randy throws rocks at him like he's a stray dog. But he just laughs and still runs for the house.

A month after Dad exploded, the car stops smouldering and Mom starts to swell. Quickly. On Monday we think she's retaining water. On Tuesday we think she's pregnant. She starts to cry. All the time. But she doesn't get any smaller with the water loss. The men stop coming around. Randy takes to orbiting the trailer again, further out in the fields and along the sewage ditches so he can't hear her crying. I take up cooking more loudly.

She's swelling. In the morning she calls me in and asks me to massage her legs. I ask her if there's money anywhere for food. She says she doesn't think so. She's run out of nylons so I rub warm tealeaves over her legs to steep them a darker colour. The men like this, she says. They'll come back now, she murmurs. In the bathroom I rub a small handful of tealeaves on my leg. The stain is peculiar. I wonder if it stains the flesh, too, or just the skin. It's hard to tell how deep things go.

Days later she can't get out of bed at all and the mattress sags, giving up a little more each day. She stops going to the bathroom, pees into a pot I bring from the kitchen, stops eating, and still she swells bigger. Randy walks to town and gets a doctor from one of the clinics. The doctor comes and opens a window in the room even though Mom will make me close it as soon as he leaves. She says mosquitoes keep getting in and they give her nightmares. The doctor tells us she needs rest. He tells us we should get out of the trailer and give her some quiet. He knows what boys can be like. But tells us we got to take good care of our mother.

I ask the doctor if she will keep growing. His head shakes slowly from side to side. He says women are a mystery. I ask how big will she get. He says he doesn't know. I keep thinking of Alice in her wonderland, drinking from the wrong bottle. This one makes you big.

A week later Randy and I can't get into Mom's room any longer. Her left leg sticks out of the bedroom door so we can't close it. We have to climb over it like a fallen tree to get to the bathroom. We don't know where her right leg has gone. When she talks now we have to listen to the wall, place a glass against it, and then holler back so she can hear us. It doesn't matter. She doesn't want anything.

Soon the aluminum sides of the trailer are bulging in the heat. At night Randy and I sleep in the yard in tents we made with blankets and the three chairs we salvaged from the kitchen. There are two small windows in her bedroom, each the size of a television. In one I can see her hair, her black, shiny hair. In the other we can see only one of her eyes. I think it might be the left one, but she's so bloated and her eye is so large and the window so small we can't tell. During the day I lean a sheet of plywood against the side of the trailer to block the sun so she won't be blinded. Randy and I sit in the dirt and shade below the window, our backs to the aluminum trailer, feeling it shudder and creak under the weight of her breath. She's stopped talking. But still we listen.

The firefighters come around again. "It doesn't look good," they say.

"They're no fucking doctors," says Randy. He heard one of the firefighters use the word and now he uses it in every sentence.

The doctor comes around again. "It doesn't look good," he says. He leaves.

"He ain't no fucking firefighter," says Randy.

The firefighters park a truck by the house and take turns hosing down the trailer. They say she must be cooking in there. The word *crisp* burns on the roof of my mouth. We're going to end up with two parents cooked. But there's nothing the firefighters can do about Mom's expanding. I think they just want to hang around and see what happens next.

At night I take the board away from the window so Mom can see the lights of the town stretching to the horizon. I like to think she can see the stars, but it's a little too bright so close to town like this. And I don't know what she can see.

It's a Tuesday night when Randy and I are wandering out in the knife grass, and he looks at me, the air crackling static between us. We run back through the grass to the trailer, stand and watch the bulging sides of it. The walls seem still, quiet, not vibrating with her breath the way they were. Down by the burning car, the firefighters have built a fire.

"That's fucking weird," says Randy.

We go around to Mom's bedroom window.

Her one eye blinks slowly. Something's happening.

"Maybe she's just tired," I say.

Randy brings around two dining room chairs and we sit facing her. I think it makes her happy that we're there. I look at Randy and I hardly recognize him. Used to be when there was nothing to do but sit around he would go apeshit from boredom.

"You know, Mom," he says to her one big eye. "You know that animals know when there's going to be an earthquake, and they run for higher ground while the people stay around and get drowned. Fucked up, eh?"

Mom's eye opens wider.

"Sorry," Randy says and looks down at the dirt. "Didn't mean to curse."

I can't stop looking at her eye. I don't say anything. I have a hard time talking to her now. I think it's because her eye doesn't focus anymore. It reminds me of when we were smaller kids and Mom took us on a road trip to the coast, to Sealand, and I was standing next to this one tank trying to find the orca. But the water was just black slate, clouds reflecting. And then there he was, floating right in front of me, quiet and calm, his one big eye watching me. I was caught in that black glass, seeing him seeing me. Scared, but not because I thought the thing was going to eat me. Scared because this one great eye was looking at me and I didn't know what he saw.

There in the back behind the trailer, sitting in front of Mom's window, the crickets out in the dark field and the smell of something barbequing on the firefighter's fire, I try to think of something to say to Mom. I can't.

We're mostly water, Randy once told me.

Sometime around midnight, the aluminum sides of the trailer give way and Mom's skin does too, like a water balloon on the pavement. With a creak and a crash, the walls split and crumple, a great wave of Mom's insides and torn parts flooding out into the yard. Randy and I are knocked back off our chairs. The wave sloshes and puts out the firefighters' fire as they knock over their lawn chairs and jog away laughing, kids playing in the waves. There in the gore and rubble, Randy looks at me. Close to pleading, I don't recognize the look at first. It's a little brother look.

The firefighters call people on their cell phones. One of them throws up in a pool of Mom at his feet. That seems disrespectful to me. That's when Randy grabs a handful of rocks and starts to run after the firefighters. He hucks rocks at them, hits one in the head, cracking a startled scream out of him. Another stands his ground, holds out his broad hand, and says, "Now look here, son," just before the next rock hits him in his front teeth, cracking one clear off. Then they are all running down the road to the highway. None of them thinks to grab the fire engine, so Randy just starts to throw rocks at it, smashing all the windows, the headlights and tail lights. One of them tries to come back for it, but Randy sees him and a rock glances off the guy's temple before he starts scrambling back down the road.

They come back for the fire engine when we are at school the next Monday. But it doesn't matter, the damage is already done.

sunflowers

Helena counts fourteen umbrellas open to dry at the back
of the church for Sunday evening service. The heavy silence
and the light clouds of incense muffle the sounds of water
dripping from nylon to marble as thunder echoes down the
long corridors.

"This thunder will take the roof off if the lightning
doesn't splinter it first," whispers Helena.

She leans forward in her seat. She doesn't kneel. Her
knees can't take it. The priest reassured her she isn't any
less faithful.

The priest sniffles ever so slightly.

Something scatters on the marble floor, and the Greek
widow, the one called Arete, looks disapprovingly at Helena.
Arete—sounds like "stop" in French and supposedly means
virtuous. This woman looks her name—each crag, every
dour line says stop, thinks Helena. She looks down to
see what's fallen from the pews. Small orange shapes on
the floor beneath her. The lentils—she keeps them in her
pockets until the right moment for the soup, but this time
she forgot to add them. Her pocket must have a tear. No
surprise the way she worries her hands, forces them deep
into pockets to keep them busy.

At the end of a sentence, the priest tries to rub his nose
on his sleeve by pointing to the statue of Christ hanging on

the west side of the cathedral. It is a quick, almost imperceptible, luminous gesture. More beautiful than the blessing of the sacrament, thinks Helena. Then Father looks up from the chalice to see if anyone saw him wipe his nose, and Helena drops her eyes in respect.

I should have brought him my soup, she thinks to herself as she sits back, once more leaking another mess of orange lentils through the gap at the back of the pew. She gathers the remaining lentils in her hand, digging around in her pocket to grasp as many of them as she can. She can't find the source of the leak, no tear, no place where the pocket gives way to her fingers. She holds her hand clasped shut in her lap, hoping not to lose any more of the lentils to the marble floor. "*Pazzesca*," she says to herself under her breath. "Why didn't you just put them in the pot?" With this, she can see Arete to her right touch her long fingers to the handkerchief she's tied around her head to cover her hair, as if to straighten everything out, set the stray hairs right and silence Helena in one gesture.

Father sniffles once more. He looks sick. He's going through the motions, pretending nothing's wrong, but she knows. He's sick. Tomorrow she'll bring him soup. She saw him earlier, down by the duck pond where he'd been out for a jog before the evening service. A cold run, his version of atonement maybe, but then this sudden storm. He must have caught the cold then. He had just finished his run, and he was bent over catching his breath. When Helena passed him, she saw how his legs had grown sleek and red with the storm, but she didn't stop. The park bench was so close, but she willed her tired feet and her aching hips to hurry, for she wanted to stop at the mission before the evening service, and if she sat, she felt sure she wouldn't get up again. But she remembered his blue shorts all the way to the mission steps.

She wanted to approach Father after the service, but what would she say? She could start by telling him about the three sunflowers she had bought in the market early this morning, but then she'd probably confess that she shops there because of the name: Constantia, Constantia Market.

"You wouldn't believe it, Father…. The name of the cross street is my middle name and the name of the market is the name of my eldest daughter. Have you ever heard of such a thing?"

He might find it funny. Something about it had amused Helena this morning as she stood there all in black purchasing those three gaudy, glorious flowers. She had to suppress a smile all the way home. "Don't get me wrong," she'd say to him. "I like this black. So simple. And it feels right to wear it, to remember Marco this way." Sometimes, though, she forgets that she's wearing these garments, finds herself humming lullabies or tunes she's heard the young ones singing while riding the bus. It isn't right.

This morning, with the flowers in hand, she'd passed that Donati widow fingering tomatoes. The one from Sicily who lives a street over from Helena's small flat. Helena didn't want to look, thought to look at the sky instead, but still turned her head just in time to catch those lines furrowed, chiselled even, in the centre of the other woman's forehead—her look of disapproval. Sunflowers. They'd always been Helena's flowers, and she'd not touched one for eleven years now, giving them only sideways glances in markets. And she wanted to tell Father all of this.

"He needs my soup," she mutters. She kisses her rosary beads and says her prayers, one for each bead, as she goes over the list of soup ingredients in her mind to see if she has left out anything else. Maybe it's not too late to add the lentils. She'll boil them in a separate pot and add them to the soup afterwards. She thinks of the sunflowers at home, turning to face the brightest light in the room, and the beads click against one another as she comforts them in her palm.

She pushes the church's front door open, and she thinks how it has always seemed to her the largest door she's ever seen. At night, when she imagines the doors of heaven in her prayers, they look something like these. Her hands are so white against the stain of the wood. Oh, her hands, their slimness, their long, delicate fingers. Every night since she was thirteen she's put cream on her hands to protect them.

Who lets you run in the rain that way, she wondered as Father stood there, bent over, catching his breath, out there in the rain. Surely there must be some place warm, there must be some place better than being out here. She turned away from him then, from the figure standing at the edge of the pond.

Then the rain began to fall harder.

"Some people are meant to be alone," the widow Mancuso had said over tea. "It's a calling."

"Yes, yes, I'm sure you're right," replied Helena. "I just think it's a little bit of a shame, him so young and all."

She will go talk to Father. He's awfully young to be a priest, and so handsome. It's taken her a while to accept him here and get used to the fact that he could be God's representative and still jog past her in the parks in the afternoon.

Nice legs. She tried to erase this thought as soon as she thought it, as soon as she saw them all wet and red in the rain, in the park. But there was something else, the way they reminded her of her Marco's legs. He'd always had wonderful legs. Oh, how she'd loved his naps in the summer, when he returned from work in the late afternoon and the heat was too unbearable to do anything but sleep. He napped and she sat in the kitchen with her feet in a big old roasting pan of cold water. She'd sneak in to watch him sleep, leaving wet footprints across the wooden floor, to see him lying on top of the blankets in his boxer shorts with those legs. Then, sitting back in the kitchen, she'd watch her footprints evaporate in the heat. She'd never told him how she thought he had the handsomest legs in the world.

When he was in the bath (oh, how he would sing, he could have been a tenor), she would find some reason to go in (Band-Aids, Aspirin, Kleenex) so she could sneak a look at his legs.

She feels too old for legs now, and a mourning woman should not have to see her confessor run by with such a pair. Who could she confess these thoughts to then? Lord, what was she supposed to do? "Forgive me, Father, for I have sinned…. I go to the parks at the same time every afternoon to see you run by. I like your blue shorts the best."

"Forgive me," she mutters.

Oh well, there are some things even God doesn't want to know.

They're only sunflowers.

She trundles home, thinking of her hands. She was thirteen when she had noticed her nana's hands, saw them all spotty and worn rough with age. In some places it looked like you could see right through them, like paper butterflies. And from that moment she grew afraid of the elements that might someday disfigure her hands in that way. And now, here they were. Her grandmother's hands. They shouldn't bother her, she thinks, since they go with the hair, the lines across her forehead, around her eyes and mouth.

And the way her back seems to curve over now, bending her towards some task she can't describe. It's her back, you see, that really torments her, makes everything else about age and loneliness seem not so bad. Oh, to have someone rub just a little ointment on the skin there, right in the small of her back. Why do they call it that, "the small of the back"? No one has touched her there for a thousand years. Since Marco. No, that's not true. The doctor has, with his cold hands and his calcium this and his stretch that. And he touched her with that cold metal disk last April when she had that cough, and asked her to inhale. She tries to think of other names for the "small of the back." How about *mesa*? Or better yet, "the dark side of Helena." Even "the valley of forgetfulness," but that's not so true, no, because she remembers Marco's fingers, the way he caressed her there when she came to him after his nap, saying, "Mother, where do you get all these muscles? Woman, you work too hard."

She'd tried growing flowers a few years after Marco died. It seemed selfish to buy them for herself, and they seemed almost indecent in the face of grief. She couldn't bear seeing them in the market and couldn't bring herself to buy them. Marco had always brought her flowers, and not just roses. He brought crazy kinds, expensive ones she half chastised him for buying because they were just starting out and could not afford them. Irises, those gaudy lilies, and sometimes even a bird of paradise. But he always knew when to get her sunflowers, knew to save them for special times. He was skilled at preserving happiness, this man with the fine legs and the occasional flowers. Helena couldn't save much, was prone to enjoying a whole box of chocolates at a sitting, so she loved how Marco taught her to hold on to some things for later.

So she'd brought old pots up from the basement, a few at a time, resting on the coarse wooden steps, and on an evening walk gathered dirt in a tattered apron and seasoned it with broken eggshells and a little compost. She bought bulbs and seeds in the market, and didn't have to smuggle them home like she did the flowers, because the seeds were so tiny and the bulbs just looked like onions or scallops. She put all the pots in the kitchen, the warmest and most moist room in the house. And no one could see in the window from the deserted lot across the alley.

But no sooner had the first bulbs sprouted, grown leaves, when the plague came. The stems and leaves thick with little green aphids. She had no idea where they had come from and no idea how to get rid of them. Perhaps she should have asked someone, the florist in the market even, but she felt embarrassed, was certain the florist would look at her black dress, her hair tied back under a black scarf, and judge her. She wanted no one to know she was wasting her time with such nonsense. She could see the widow Donati's lips, her furrowed forehead. She thinks to herself, now really, that Francesca Donati could wear black underwear and eat only black things and all that mourning wouldn't change the fact that her husband had skinny legs and thin lips that never spoke a good word.

Now my Marco, she thinks to herself. Well, he was a good man. She had loved him, and loved him just a little more when he went to work each day. When he retired and stayed around the house, collecting those damn stamps,

then, Lord forgive her, she loved him just a little less.
He hadn't collected them until he retired, and then he
went crazy for them, and it didn't seem he was going about
it the way a stamp collector should. There was no carefulness to what he did, and she still finds stamps in the oddest
places. Sometimes she wanders through the pockets of his
clothes where they still hang on his side of the closet, and
there she often finds stamps, and sometimes coins.

Strangest of all, she once found four stamps from
Amsterdam stuck to the inside of his shaving kit cover.
Rich with colour and almost garish, they wanted to tell
a story. Were they the cost of some love letter he once
received? Or one he never sent? They were pretty, that's
true. Perhaps they were never for sending and he just put
them there so he could see them all the time. Perhaps.

When he told her he was going to retire, she thought,
Well, I'll have less time to myself but maybe, just maybe,
I will get to know this man who sleeps on the right side
of the bed. When he finally did retire, it was as if a stranger
had moved in, a different man, and day by day he grew
more and more like a secret, took up habits she couldn't
explain. He went to the park for part of the afternoon and
she'd see him there sometimes, but all he ever did was feed
the birds and sit on the park bench, saying hi to the babies
as they went by in prams.

Maybe, she thought, he misses our children, misses the
early years when he was working too hard. He did call the
kids more, it seemed, called them even more than she did.
Would sit in the hallway on the phone, ask them about the
weather and their cars. They weren't extraordinary conver-
sations. He didn't learn anything new. But they would buoy
his evening, have him carrying around smiles for the rest

of the night. She didn't call them as much. She was trying to let them get on with their lives. In the park she'd watch him from a distance and wouldn't approach him. She didn't go to the park with him because he didn't ask. She was just glad he was out of the house, mostly.

She thinks now that some people aren't meant to retire, that it was wrong for such a man as her Marco to have so much time on his hands, and she wonders if he was unhappy. What had made him retire? Had he thought he'd get to know her better? Well, he was resting now and it was all worth it, *caro mio*, if his final years with his stamps from Amsterdam and his babies in the park made things more restful.

Those years, those final years with him, she'd just kept to her routine: breakfast, making the beds, the market, some errands, a little cleaning, each afternoon a different room, then dinner. But she didn't make his lunch for work anymore. It was only after he died that she changed the way she did things, that she herself decided to retire. There were the bulbs, but they failed and died in brown splotches from all the aphids, so she wrapped them up gently in newspaper and threw them out. Now, years later, she finally allows herself to make trips to the fresh flower market down on 53rd, and feels good about it, even though she'll sometimes go blocks out of her way if she thinks she can avoid running into the Donati widow. To camouflage the flowers, she asks the florist to wrap them in plain paper, in tight bundles even though he protests that they won't be able to breathe. But no matter. They still look like a bunch of flowers.

They remain fresh if she gives them clean water every couple of days. And then that's that. It's such a shame to have them for so little time. She wants to be buried in a bed of sunflowers, but doesn't know whom to tell this to. Her children all expect she will want to be dressed in black, her hair drawn back in a bun, smoothed from her forehead. They will probably have the man at the funeral home put that awful makeup on her, the way they put it on Marco. All that artistry to pretend she's not as dead. And Lord, it would take that stucco paste to fill the lines across her forehead. What's the point? But sunflowers. She wants to walk up to those doors, those gates to heaven, with long, white fingers holding sunflowers, and she wants Marco to see her then, in that moment, as the doors open and she and the flowers lean towards the light.

It takes some time to boil the lentils. "*Donna stupida*," she says to herself over and over. She moves towards the stove and in her mind checks off a list of the ingredients to make sure she hasn't forgotten anything today. She's added more pepper and garlic than usual—these will cure Father of what ails him. Maybe he won't run today, with the rain, with his cold. But just in case, she thinks. Just in case. It must be difficult for him. Men aren't made to live alone. When she turns from the stove she sees the sunflowers, droopy, gangly, and brilliant, and pauses to smile at them.

She digs to the back of the cupboard to find Marco's old work thermos. The plastic has cracked in a few places, but when she fills it with warm water, seals it shut, and holds it upside down, it doesn't leak. It will do. It won't keep the soup warm for long, but he can reheat it. She can't bring herself to meet him at the church, to bring the soup there—that's not the kind of confession she's planned. She decides to bump into him near the lagoon. "What a coincidence!" she'll say as she pulls the soup from the canvas bag hung over her arm.

She chooses the park bench at the last bend in the path before it cuts up to the church from the lagoon. There's a light rain, so she takes a plastic bag from her coat pocket and stretches it out to sit upon. She sits down under her biggest black umbrella and looks out over the water, where little birds move from shelter to shelter. She occasionally looks over her shoulder to see if Father is approaching in his blue shorts. She hasn't seen him running much, and she wouldn't know his routine at all if she hadn't overheard him talking to one of the young men in the parish about the importance of exercise, how he runs every other day.

The rain is falling harder now, and she catches a glimpse of him running from the trees alongside the lagoon. He should sprint back to the church and the mission, but he stops right there, beside the water in the middle of the park. Helena practises in her mind, "What a coincidence," but she can't move from the bench. Maybe he will see her and begin the conversation. It isn't a big lagoon, and on the other side there are various people running for the shelter of trees, or to the cafés across the street from the park. Still he stands there.

Helena slowly puts the canvas bag over her arm and stands, her right hip still wanting to sit, and then she shambles carefully past him, lowering her umbrella to hide her face, using the black edge as a veil. Then the rain begins to fall even harder, as if to say something, as if to offer up some message. She turns back to see if he is running again, but her breath catches, she stops. Watches him as he walks up to the edge of the pond, drenched now, looking down at the water's edge like he might jump in. She thinks to call out, because the widow Mancuso had told her that some children playing in that water had gotten a disease from all those ducks. But she doesn't call out.

Standing there, watching him in his blue shorts, she knows he would understand about the sunflowers. A sin not to leave him alone. She nods softly to herself. It's rude to stare, so she starts home again, tilting the umbrella to hide her face.

flamenco

Listless Thursday, a clutter of old men at the back bar watch sports they've never played televised on muted screens. Closer to the small square of stage, the table loungers lean famished and bored. She sits poised against the wall, her eyes cast down on the stage spread out around her feet. The man with the guitar, his dark hair falling over his face, oblivious to her, knows what comes next despite her slanted repose. A woman waiting.

She's pulled to her feet like she's already lost this tug of war, but then fights the floor, the crack of her heels, the wood floor run smooth and tan where other women like her have eroded the black paint. Our glasses half full, the waitress folding paper napkins, the bartender watching soccer on a small TV below the bar. A breeze leans through the wide-open café windows but then steps back into the noise of the traffic, lets the sleepy heat have its way. Drowned faces in passing cars wash downriver, see her on this tired small stage, see her with her arms above her head, her face now thrown back, a trap almost sprung, pulsing, her feet thundering a counterpoint.

The singing old man doesn't know he's old. He sings like he did when he was twenty-one. It's all he can do. All he can do not to think about later and the empty chairs. Not even a forgotten purse to ask him what the words mean and who he is singing for.

On the sidewalk outside, a man in a white tank top stops. Sediment of tattoos, he leans against the street sign and smokes a cigarette, pretends she is not dancing. Pretends he's upwind, not down, longed for, biting his bottom lip, tasting his woman's anger. But he doesn't know her. Looks like he might stare down the traffic. Doesn't stand a chance, but I root for him.

— — —

This story is about what they can't see. How in that skinned open space between tables her hands ignore her face as they unfold origami the closed mouths of birds, her arms all slender throat, reaching up above her now, high above the floor, her hands face then turn away. Equal parts want and beleaguer.

My phone rings, you calling, so I take it out to the street. It's a poor connection, the kind where every word I say echoes back. It's impossible to love this way.

wabi sabi

In the village across the strait, there's an old woman named Alice who shapes clay by hand, a careful hand. Makes the strongest clay pots on the coast, so strong they can be dropped from great heights, can be sat upon like chairs by hefty men, can be bounced off walls, leave the plasterboard wounded, and spin careless with disregard and tumble. Strong and still, waiting to break without explanation, waiting to pour over into contradiction and shatter across plank floors, living a shorter life than they should.

The end is in the beginning, she tells the rag of a cat that keeps her company amongst the clay. The half-life of pottery. She sees each pot's end, the various drops and falls, those that will crack open in the heat like dried-out seed pods, those that will shatter at night and spill water into puddles for the cat to walk through and leave tracks on the kitchen floor. Each of her pots or plates will find its necessary breaking point and shatter into something else, moth to caterpillar, turn from pots into bowls, from bowls to spoons, a diminishing afterlife for dishes. A reminder to startled women in kitchens and on porches that even the most careful life can break, can change in a moment.

Alice was only eleven when her mother died one Thursday, full of wanting and regret, in the trailer park on the hill. The neighbours said Alice's mother was muttering as she removed the blocks from under the trailer's wheels and lay down in front of them with a wrong smile; she barely cried out when the trailer began to roll and crush her, ever so slowly. She couldn't have been happy, married to that man, said some of the wives. What fisherman's wife is happy, whispered the others to themselves along the rows of trailers.

— — —

They couldn't stop the trailer once it started rolling. It was a slow roll. By Saturday it had reached the last row of the trailer court and was on its way down the street to the water. Alice's father just shook his head, asking aloud, "How does a woman get crushed under something so slow?" Alice sat in the corner, a pale, wide face, the question staining her.

Just two days later, Alice and her father were getting used to coming home to a different address each night. The other fishermen offered to share blocks, to help stop the trailer, but her father gently shook his head, no. They could see the water now. It seemed like a deadline. All the neighbours agreed that the trailer would surely stop rolling before it reached cannery row and the ocean. Her father, though, simply watched the waves on the bay from the living room, watched as they drew closer, so quiet Alice could hear the gravel grind underneath the determined trailer. Trailers ain't meant to move, said one of the fishermen with gristle in his tone, intending for her to pass this on to her father, to put some sense into him. She and the fisherman watched the slow turn of the wheel and nodded as she realized he wasn't joking.

That night Alice found her father standing in the kitchen, looking at all the open cupboard doors. Suddenly, without breath, angry with wheels and trailers and chipped-edged wives that became what they shouldn't, he smashed every dish in the kitchen. Alice stood in the doorway looking out over the shards and dust of every dish rendering the kitchen topographic. She looked down at the rubble as he slumped over the sink, looking out at the village passing slowly by. She knelt down, picked up a dish shard. They say this was the moment she became enamoured with certainty.

— — —

Until she grew up and met her own fisherman. Stories repeat themselves, a riddle looking for an answer. They say her husband was a mean man, gristle and bone with lost razors in the sock drawer and unforgiving edges. This life she'd not planned for caught her unawares, so the story told her instead. She did foresee that night when he grew jealous of the way her hands touched clay, the night after all the other nights she had avoided touching his bristled, hairy skin. The night he'd come home, a jagged path, mouth full of sweet-rot liquor, falling to the walls, his anger so loud—she kept glancing out the windows to see who could hear. Then he lurched for the back door, the backyard, the kiln shack, where she threw clay and fired the pots. Back door, backyard, kiln shack, and her hair stopped growing at once, for she knew where his jealousy took him. He broke every unbreak-able pot, shattered their small mouthfuls of certainty. The impossible breaking into small bits of the possible.

In the morning, Alice stood in the doorway to the kiln shack and looked across the floor at the broken crockery. She looked down at her hands that were smaller then, the hands of a six-year-old. Her hands didn't answer. She found him snoring in pools of his own bile and urine on the weeping porch. She bent down to his sun-bleached edges, reached out her hands, placing them around his neck. She placed them firmly, water against ocean floor; she touched him as though he were clay, though stubborn and impure, clay she had to prepare.

When the sun rose up, her man of gristle and bone woke to find bits of flesh strewn on the tired wood planks of the porch around him, a few of his edges rounded. He was hairless now, smooth. His features rounder. She saw him through the kitchen window, watched him waking up, and she was sad to see he had lost some of his handsomeness, rounder as he was. He wasn't the man she married. She watched him looking penitent, or maybe just hungover, as he hosed his bits off the porch. The seagulls swooped down, crying out, fighting over his pieces. And then they flew away, and she and he settled into a new quiet.

He didn't go out drinking that night, but stayed home and even glazed the few new pots she'd made that morning. She pressed harder into the clay, found a thickness to the walls of the pots she'd never found before, discovering more unbreakable certainty. And he didn't go out the next night. She came home from the market to find him on the couch with her crochet hook, improvising doilies. He used the word "grace," said doilies were little flat pieces of grace. They were lopsided, gap toothed, and hideous. But they were a start.

On the third night, up to her elbows in the kitchen sink, she saw through the window the deep sea fishing boats returning on the horizon, saw him stand and take shaky, newborn steps to the edge of the porch. She didn't call out, just sank down in the sinkwater, placed her palms on the bottom, her hair falling forward to shroud her. He was gone from the porch before the boats docked.

Later that night, she waited on the stoop. Down in the village, the fishermen drank and carried on like thunder, like traffic on a bridge. She waited until the fishermen wandered home, slurred and staggered. Her fisherman, sick and infected and full of quick edges. Hardly a blurry breath before he lurched through living room, back door, backyard, kiln shack.

She did not follow. She waited on the porch, hoping these pots would hold their own. Then, as she heard the shattering cries of each pot, she flinched little griefs as each capillary nerve burnt out in the salt night air.

Morning, she found him once again, wheezing, damp on the sagging porch where it lurched above the muskeg. In the crisp morning air, she reached out with her two hands and placed them around his ridged and bent-to-purpose neck. She began again, kind, the way she was with flawed clay. Smaller clumps of him fell to the porch as she worked out the impurities, the air bubbles.

In the morning she awoke to peaches in the air, and found him in the kitchen making impressionistic waffles, a wounded apology on his lips. He was smaller now, shorter than her, and several kinds of sorry. In the afternoon, she saw him crocheting ragged, wandering doilies, a grim frustration pinching his forehead. Later, near dusk, she caught him on the porch, muttering, found him unsure where he was headed or what he was going to do next. He was sleepless, an all-over itch.

Two nights later he came home spun and slurred again, in the kiln shack before she could put on her housecoat. She sat at the kitchen table, listening to the shattering, waiting. She found him there, crashed into the boards. She picked up the broom and dustpan, and carefully swept the shards of the too-soon-broken into small piles around his drooling, heaving breaths. Then she leaned down over him, her hands now comfortable against the bare skin of his sunburned neck. She set to work once more, still not ready to abandon this clay. Smaller edges of him scattered across the floor like eraser.

Three nights later, she stood at the kitchen window again, her hands treading dishwater. She heard a rusty squeak as her husband rose from the porch swing, saw him step into the frame of the kitchen window and place his ragged doily on the porch railing. The other fishermen were coming up the path from the bay, looking to bring him back to the smoked salmon, the faded girly posters in the engine room, the canning jars full of rum and fish scales.

She lowered her head and looked at her hands in the dishwater. She looked back at him, framed by the kitchen window, three days' worth of saved pots out back, waiting. She watched as her husband took a step towards the edge of the porch, the sun emerging from behind him like he was a passing cloud. She had to shade her eyes with the back of one wet hand.

She watched as his head toppled off his neck and bounced down the steps to the feet of his friends. Her husband's head looked up at them, startled, a broken pleading. And then his face relaxed and looked almost philosophical, as though he now understood. The other fisherman screamed in a very ungristled way, a scream that brought the village women to their own sagging porches.

Perhaps it was the smile. Maybe one of the friends had seen her smiling in the kitchen window, and that was why he ran three miles to the next village to get the only local constable. But there was no weapon, no explanation, only her lack of grief. That's not and never will be enough to convict a fisherman's wife.

Later that night, Alice listened to the wind whistle through the broken shingles on the roof, and she listened for his footsteps on the reluctant porch. She listened to the front door not opening, heard him not shouting at her carefulness, not jealous anymore of the kindness and care she shaped into the pottery. She even sniffed the air, not smelling of peaches and apology.

Then she heard it. A bone-splitting thunder crack. The dishes, the bowls, the vases, the jugs, popcorned, staccato, and startling. She sat up in bed, slowly. He's done it again, she thinks. He's broken the unbreakable.

And from that day forward, none of her works would last more than a week. She tried different clay, black clay from as far south as she could find it. Grey clay, speckled like a cormorant egg, from a valley near the hot springs where the coastal mountains meet the Rockies. She threw the clay harder, then more gently, but none of it mattered. Each night, on their bed, her back to the window, she could feel the air between the bedroom window and the kiln shack slack thinner. Inevitable. Yet a careful design in the break-age, how the bowls became cups, the cups became spoons, and the spoons' sparkle smashed into handfuls of crystalline sand. Nothing for her to do but shape the largest bowls she could fashion.

Some said she was cursed, tormented by her husband's ghost. Some predicted she would grow poor and crazy, but her bowls sold more than they ever had. Fishermen all along the ragged coast would wake up to hangovers and see a bowl or vase on the windowsill where there had been none. If these shattered days later, the fishermen would remember how husbands, like bowls, can break, and they would know they were living on borrowed time. They would watch nervously as their wives moved from room to room with smiles as careful as commas, and they'd have a momentary sense of their own delicate breaking point.

seeds

The nursery owners give Kevin Sunday off. It wasn't entirely his fault. On Saturday he was carrying a tray of mums, concise explosions of glee, and he couldn't stop looking at their open faces. His toe caught on the lip of track where the glass doors roll open and shut, and, in the moment he was falling, he realized he was going to fall on top of the mums. So he threw the tray out from under him and fell forehead first onto the edge of one of the planting tables.

The owners clustered around him, touching his forehead, running for ice, the first-aid kit, cooing with worry, but he wanted to make sure the mums were okay. They thought he must be in shock. Maybe he was. But he wanted to make sure the mums were okay. Alec wouldn't let him get up, blocked his way. He didn't mean to shove Alec, the tall owner. Then both owners were there, holding their hands out in front of themselves, palms towards him, talking more softly. Kevin took deep breaths. They gave him a stool to sit on, handed him a glass of water. Then one of them carefully stuck a Band-Aid on Kevin's forehead where he had scratched himself. Look at that bruise already, the one said while the other covered his mouth.

Plants are something Kevin knows. From third grade, when all the students planted seeds but Kevin's grew twice as tall, he knew. People don't look at plants the way he does.

He can see this in the way they manhandle trays of gladiolas, plop them in their station wagon trunks, the way their fingers fumble through tomato stalks, their faces pretending they know what they are feeling, fingers mute. They don't know that to truly know a tomato plant you need to meet it with your face, you need to smell it.

He knows seeds, too. To most people, seeds are unremarkable, except for the rare ones, peculiar, like sunflower seeds. Kevin can identify any seed, can sense in each its hankering to be the hibiscus or carrot it will become. He knew enough to get a job at the nursery just off Main. He also knows that the owners deliberately keep him out back, don't want him too near the customers. He's okay with that. Used to it, even. Seems the same people who try to smell with their fingers also talk a lot, and Kevin can only stare, the words exploding around him like dandelion fluff kicked into the air.

He gets Mondays off. He mostly likes to stay home, but every Monday he makes himself go to the café on the corner, have a coffee, and pretend to read the newspaper. It's a way to be closer to people, closer than the back room at the nursery but without all the words. Even from across the café, without hearing their voices, Kevin can see this man with his hands in his lap and his desperation to stay, and that woman with one leg kicked back under the chair, only her toe touching the ground, her desperation to leave. He can see that the old man with the worn shoes has only a few words, but they are all for lonely. Sometimes Kevin wonders what it means, this ability to read people so clearly, that maybe he's supposed to help them with his knowledge in some way. Tell the man with the worn shoes that there's a woman, the one with the glasses lost in her grey curls, who watches him some days from a table outside on the sidewalk. Maybe someday, he thinks.

They are kind, the owners. They put up with a lot, Kevin thinks. They gave him Sunday off to recover. But now it doesn't feel like Sunday should. Kevin decides the only thing to be done with an unexpected Sunday is to pretend it is a Monday. But the sidewalks are clogged with people not going places, just standing and talking, and the café is sheet-lightning laughter and words, faces jammed against faces. In the café line, Kevin laughs, thinks of the tray of mums. He orders his coffee, but it's a boy behind the counter, not the Monday morning caramel-on-a-windowsill girl.

What? The boy doesn't hear him ask for a coffee.

You mean pardon, says Kevin.

What? The guy glints at a girl three people back.

Kevin says it louder, Coffee.

The guy rings it in, talking to the barista about that bottle of vodka last night, holds out his hand without looking at Kevin. It's not a Monday.

Every chair in the café is taken. Kevin tries to focus, to see if anyone looks like they might be close to finishing their food, might be packing up their stuff. Then a young couple in the corner stand, reach for their jackets, and Kevin is in the woman's chair before she's even put an arm in a sleeve. They smile at him, but Kevin knows this smile, knows it means he's done things just a little off again. But he has a table.

Safe.

Still, the spoon against glass clinks, the scream of the espresso machine, the avalanche of words burying the room. Kevin has to strain to focus. Then the bells above the door tinkle. A mother and her child. Kevin feels like he's looking into a mirror. He and the boy both have a Band-Aid on their forehead. They see one another and both start a little, the boy stopping in his tracks so the mother has to drag him through the door into the café. In the same moment, the child points at Kevin's Band-Aid and Kevin touches his forehead in surprise.

Two weeks before at the doctor's, Kevin had removed his shirt as the doctor asked, and looked up at the ceiling to avoid the doctor's stare. He'd run his fingers over his own body, pointing to the places where a spider had bitten him.

"Yes, no worries, I can see them," said the doctor. But Kevin felt he had to show him each one, in case he missed them, his fingers running Braille over his own body. Kevin didn't look at the doctor's face looming over him. Instead he looked at the picture of a tropical beach that had been stapled to the ceiling.

In the café, the child still points at Kevin, then reaches up and touches his own Band-Aid, to be sure he really has one too, like he wonders if he imagined his own fall in the living room at home, the cartoon Band-Aid his mother found in the mess of bottles and old toothbrushes in the bathroom drawer. Maybe he never fell, never cut his fore-head, and maybe his mother hadn't berated him for being so clumsy as she roughly put the Band-Aid over the wound. She'd kissed the Band-Aid, an afterthought, something the mother thought a good mother should do. Kevin can see it all, even the colour of the shag carpet in the living room. He wants to tell the boy that it did happen. It isn't a story some other person, a man in a café with a similar bandage, tells you.

Kevin realizes that this is a sign. This boy with the same wound. This is what he was called to do. And in this moment, everything he will do has already happened, and the rest will be like recounting it to a stranger, as though it were already done. This is why he was given this ability, why he can see the child so clearly, his hand on the hem of his mother's jacket, the mother's Formica grief.

Sitting at the table, he waits for the spaces, the tiny bouts of time measured in breath, like gasps. When she turns away from the child to look at the olives and eggs floating in glass jars on the café counter, he feels the first gasp. The child looks across at him then, and points to Kevin's Band-Aid again, in recognition. The mother turns back and places her hand on top of the child's head, so he looks away in that moment and up into his mother's eyes. She takes a second to glance in Kevin's direction, but Kevin anticipates this, knows she's aware of him sitting there, so he turns away, though he's loathe to turn his eyes away from the boy for even a moment.

The man at the counter asks what she would like, so she turns back and leans over towards the man to be heard above the din of the café. She takes her hand from the boy's head to balance herself on the chrome counter. Free from his mother's hand, the boy turns to look at Kevin again. He waves a little with his right hand, and Kevin smiles but doesn't wave back—he doesn't want to draw attention to himself. But the child won't stop waving so Kevin waves back, a small wave.

There it is. Another gasp. It begins with a roar through his ears, the hungry-bee words in the air slowing their wings, muted, the hands of the hummingbird blue-haired woman at the next table treading water now, gently. Some other power tells Kevin to move, to reach out to the child, to save him from his mother's creased grimace and well-seasoned grief. The boy will know seeds, and Kevin can show him how tomato plants reek a face full of thirst or happiness or heat exhaustion. How he will breathe it in, too. The weight of a river pushes at Kevin's back.

The child's mother turns back from the counter, crouches down, turns the child towards her, and removes his jacket so he won't overheat in the crowded café, the windows fogged up with the humidity of the day. She kisses him on the forehead, unconscious, the way she brushes his hair from his eyes more frequently as the need for a haircut increases. The child doesn't seem to mind that she only touches him to make sure he's still there.

Kevin sees all this, and he sees what she would never say out loud. Her love for him like eight lives given up to live one. That the reason she has the boy clean up his toys and put them in the chest everyday at four o'clock is that she can't stand the resemblance, how she sees herself in the chaos splayed out all over the playroom floor.

Kevin turns back to the newspaper on the table and flips the pages, eyes narrowed with intent, pretending to look at the pictures, just as the mother turns to look his way again. This will be easy, he thinks. He watches the mother and child out of his peripheral vision to make sure they don't leave the café without him.

She folds his jacket over her arm, stands up, and looks around the café for a good place to sit, away from the windows where the cigarette smoke from outside leaks in. Last time she brought her son here he got a headache. Not that he complained. He hardly ever says anything. He isn't the sort of child who complains or whines, but she can read the headache in the small crease that forms between his little eyebrows, the beginnings of what will be a frown later in life, she thinks. Maybe it will make him look distinguished. Or maybe just tense. So this time she sits them further away from the door and watches his open face for signs of tension.

His father's eyes. But she doesn't like to think like that. No good can come from raising a child with memories that aren't his own.

She turns, then notices how her son keeps looking in the direction of the man reading a newspaper, even notices the Band-Aid on the man's face. But she doesn't make the small leap to how the child might be interested in someone with the same Band-Aid on his forehead in the same place. Instead she feels a pang, the absence of men in the boy's life, partly because it's the safest way to think about the lack of men in her own life. She figures the boy must be interested in this man with a newspaper, reads his interest as longing for a father figure. Then she checks herself, thinks of her own father and smiles— does the child really need someone to hold back his love and not express emotions? Maybe.

She shows the child how to dip the hard biscotti into his hot chocolate, and he likes that. He turns back to the table and away from the man with the newspaper. But the boy is a little too excited and slops hot chocolate on the black table.

From where Kevin sits, he can only see the mother and son if he looks sideways, too obvious. He contemplates moving his chair so he won't be facing their direction, but he is sure he'll draw attention to himself that way. So he opts to focus on his periphery and tries to guess when the mother might notice him looking. Of course, he misjudges a little; she catches his glance once or twice, but he just scatters his look across the various heads in the café then rests his eyes on the passing traffic outside, furrowing his forehead, pretending pensive.

Kevin sees the child spill his hot chocolate and the look of frustration on the mother's face as she jumps up and frets to the counter in search of more napkins or a cloth. The blood rushes to his head, the roaring sound of a gasp. He has walked to the door, turned to the boy who watches him. Kevin points at the Band-Aid on his own forehead and smiles.

The mother grabs napkins from the small metal dispenser at the counter. The café owner flashes to her, perturbed.

"Spill something?" He looks at her like she's making a mess.

"Yes, my son—"

"I'll give you a cloth. Here, let me take those for you," he says as he reaches for the napkins. She offers them back, knowing her hand has been slapped. She lowers her head ever so slightly.

"I'm sorry," she says. "He's just a little clumsy. He gets excited, that's all. Loves his chocolate."

She turns back to the table then, sees the spilled chocolate, sees her son's empty seat. She blinks, a pounding, a gasp, a roar filling her ears. She turns towards the door, but has to turn the world before she can turn her head, rigid with panic. She sees him, her son, his hand in the hand of some man walking away from the café, her son looking over his shoulder at her, smiling, waving, leaving her. Then they turn the corner.

It is the smile that staples her to the floor. Her son was smiling, not worried, holding a stranger's hand and leaving her. Like she was never his mother. Happy. And leaving her.

As she sits in the police station talking to the officer, she recites the events, frustrated with the questions, frustrated because nothing but the smile matters.

Forty feet away in a holding cell, Kevin tries to focus on the crack in the concrete, tries to imagine a blade of grass growing up and through. He knows plants could move buildings, if pressed to.

They ask him why. They ask him if he likes little boys, if he thinks about little boys naked. And they ask him how he possibly thought he could escape with the boy with a whole café of witnesses. He says to them that no one was watching. He's frustrated with their questions, frustrated because they can't understand. They didn't see. Sundays are so different than Mondays.

Months later, walking in a mall, she sees him walking towards her and her son, and she clutches the boy to her, so fiercely she'll later find bruises along his shoulders where her fingers crushed him, though he does not make a noise. But the man just walks on by and the boy just looks up at her, confused. A small part of her in shock wonders if she imagined the whole thing.

undertow

They fall asleep after sex in the light of an afternoon that
disarms the clock. Kate wakes up with sand in her belly
button, looks up and sees in the high windows of the basement apartment the many legs passing behind the blinds.
She sees his eyes are blue, not the grey they looked outside
the corner store. The late-afternoon light seems to reach
her through fathoms and fathoms of water.

They fall asleep. He tells her the sand comes from the
extra blanket he threw on the bed, one he used at the
beach. It's the kind of blanket one would use for a picnic,
so she wonders if he went to the beach on a picnic with
someone else. She feels the grit of the sand with her index
finger and thumb, and imagines she's way down deep,
drowned on a Sunday.

They fall asleep, and when she wakes up this time his
back is to her, so she places her chin on his arm and catches
a half-glimpse of his face. Small flutter of eyelashes, she sees
that he is awake.

He says something under his breath. She can't hear what
it is. The water weighs upon them, the pressure immense,
so they have to move slowly.

— — —

Kate is on her way to the store for a litre of milk. Perhaps
a few flowers. The corner market usually has a selection,

if they survive the chill rain of this morning. She arrives to find them bedraggled, the lilies embarrassed, the irises long since open. There is little occasion this morning except that Mark is away, the dog needs to be walked, and the rain has slicked the city a darker pallor of grey. The whole world is underwater. She spent the morning padding quietly from room to room, the shadows half comfortable, and she was reluctant to turn on the lights in their small brick townhouse.

Perhaps he won't call tonight. Perhaps he will forget to call during this trip. Last February he was in Florida and so busy he'd been unable to call. She imagined then that he was having an affair. Even now she can see the woman's hair, how she wears it in the morning as she drinks her coffee, holds the cup with both hands like in TV commercials. Her eyes are blue and her hair is brown. She has delicate hands that keep her long hair impossibly straight and, with a con-ductor's languid simplicity, can even calm eddies and clear away the sidewalk detritus where she walks. Kate always seems to be falling apart. She regularly finds bits of paper in her hair, food her distracted fingers left behind; she stumbles on pavement stones and sinkholes find her, blindside her on a simple, fall-strewn Sunday. She has mastered the appear-ance, the illusion of containment—the face of calm hiding the loose pocket threads. Delicate training, this learning to look placid, porcelain under the duress of much pain. Kate loves this woman in her own way. She is the woman Kate wants to be for him.

In the grocery store, the bell above the door catches her between skim and one percent, a dairy-fat debate velcroed to her mind under the glaring fluorescent lights. She reaches for the one percent, feels the cold dew on the outside of the carton, and places it in the crook of her arm. She turns towards the cashier while absently wondering if the dog has found shelter from the rain under the awning of the store where she tied him. At the cash register she fumbles with wet fingers sticking in her denim pockets, searching for lost change.

She notices this man then, walking towards the counter, notices how the morning wears him with a shadow of a Sunday beard, and she finds herself imagining the smell of him, musky in his yesterday clothes. Perhaps it's the grey cut of his eyes, or the way his T-shirt sags at the neckline, exposing his clavicles. There is something vulnerable about him. She has to leave the store and walk out into the haggard morning. Riley, the dog, cowers under the eaves, waiting for her with a hurt and almost hopeful expression, the hair above his eyes and on his paws soaked down. She wants to look back through the decaled door, past the posters for concerts that have already happened. She wants to see what he's buying. He probably lives somewhere nearby, she thinks. Some place warm and dry.

She teeters, one brink step from walking out into the rain, to walk the parks until she is drenched. She has done it before. She doesn't know where this mad tic comes from, just that she sometimes yields to it and tells no one. She should go home for the dog's sake, towel him dry and wrap him up in a blanket by the foot of the bed, but she realizes she is waiting just outside the shelter of the eaves, feeling tendrils of hair soak to her temples, her forehead. She can't move. Maybe home isn't so homey anymore, or maybe she's slipped on some subtle gap, some crack in the pavement, so that now she will never go back. Slip on a crack, never go back. She has these days.

— — —

But what about the dog? He is hardly her dog, more Mark's, really, and if she were to leave she would want to leave everything. She doesn't hate Mark. It's just that most weekends he is in town he hardly leaves the house, and he has a way of filling the rooms with newspaper shuffling, dissonant humming, bellowing out to her across the length of the apartment, sonar for water buffalos. Bellowing so that she feels driven out into the morning in search of coffee or milk or some missing staple. Now, even though he is out of town, he fills the place, as though he might suddenly walk into the room with a coffee cup in hand, wearing only some old grey T-shirt. The sight of his thighs and his penis peeking out from under the shirt used to seem sweet to her, but lately she finds herself turning away, pretending distraction, pretending she doesn't see him. She hates herself for being so fickle, hates how she only falls in love with him again whenever he has his hair cut and she can see the tender nape of his neck again.

She knows the man from the corner store will soon open the door, and she braces herself for the sound of the bell, imagines the *ding* so that when he opens the door she won't appear startled. She plans to turn to him and smile to see if he says anything. It's a gamble. She will not speak; she will wait for his word. And if he says nothing, she will go home, perhaps.

Hers is the spirit of infinite hope, and she has the scars to prove it. Those scars from her childhood and all those years in the house among the orchards. It was the place of her childhood, and it occupies all the memories of her youth. The house, the orchard, both somewhere on the other side of the country and her parents now dead, unable to challenge what she remembers.

What she remembers: mud, hay dust, tadpoles like erotic

punctuation in the pond shallows, carcasses of foxes when the thresher cleared the field, the loneliness of a childhood in the mountains with only the orchards, two dogs, and her parents. Some summers, with the absence of school, she would go for whole months without seeing another child. Then she would play in the trees, dreaming of tree houses and imagining friends to fill them.

— — —

Her parents let her build in the north orchard since those trees were not as productive, and the fruit crop less hearty. They knew the tree house would damage the tree, perhaps even kill it since Kate secured the structures with nails pounded directly into the tree's flesh. Her parents could not offer any other way to secure the planks, since neither of them were very good with their hands. And so they gave these trees to Kate.

This lack of dexterity is perhaps all that Kate inherited from them. By the end of the summer, six tree houses had fallen to their deaths, the strongest lasting well into the night before it crashed to the earth, frightening them all from their beds.

It was late summer when she gave up on trees—gravity seemed too reliably unreliable. She carried the broken pieces of the past six tree houses to the north end of the orchard, furthest from the house, and walked further then, into the fields beyond the orchard. It was mid-summer and the fields had not yet been hayed, so she had to make a foundation that pressed the grass down and away from the structure. Kate's mother was relieved, though unsure that a tree house could still be a tree house built on the ground. Since she no longer had to fear how far her daughter could fall, however, she let the definition slide.

The structure Kate built took the shape of a pyramid, or, as she would later describe it, a wooden teepee. It had to lean on itself and the ground since there were no trees to hold it up, so she used up all the nails in her father's ice cream bucket, insistent that they would hold and that this one would weather the elements. And it did. One day. Two days. Three. After a week her mother said she could sleep there overnight. In the mountains, summer nights were short with an extended dusk and dawn, so her mother could see her through the half-light from the house and know that she was safe.

— — —

Did Kate remember these tree shanties, or were her memories the products of years of hearing her mother tell the stories to friends at dinner parties? It didn't matter if the tree house stories from her childhood were true. It was this story, the last one, about the wooden teepee which she didn't need verified, for the evidence runs from just below her right shoulder down towards the middle of her back, stopping just before the ridge of muscle that borders the bumps of her spine. She'd been scarred that night she'd slept out in the tree house on the ground when she rolled over in her sleep and accidentally bumped the sloping wall at a point of weakness, so it fell with a hush and a crash on top of her. Her mother heard her scream through the open windows, through the fly screens, ran out into the starlit night, her bare feet slapping the path's chill muddiness. She ran as fast as she could through the north orchard, stubbing her toes on the wandering roots of the crippled trees and slipping on the fallen, crushed apples.

   She drove Kate to the hospital and stayed with her, watching the doctor lean over the child's delicate back, thread the needle in and out of her punctured skin. She later described how wrong it was to see this creature of racing breath and light stranded and still on the white paper bed. The T-shirt Kate had been sleeping in was torn and soaked with blood where the rows of nails had bitten through the flesh. Lurid.

Kate knew all this from the versions of the story her mother would later tell. She'd cap it with a moral. Something about the animal strength of mothers, adding how Kate's father, who had always vomited at the sight of blood, stayed home riding waves of nausea. Only once did her mother tell the real ending. How the doctor took her mother into the hallway, his hands fidgeting with something metal in his blue scrub pockets. How he told her that Kate was fine and that she'd need nine stitches. It was the word for the thread holding Kate's folds of skin together, it was the word "stitches," that made her faint then, and helped her punctuate the doctor's sentence as she crumpled to the floor. She only bumped her head. She didn't need any stitches there.

— — —

Door chimes startle Kate, despite her best plans. From where the man stands outside the corner store he can't see any of the scars. Him, with his hesitant turn-and-look-over-the-shoulder smile, the pound of coffee beans in his left hand, and the way Riley leans in and smells his crotch. The rain falls off the eaves, a curtain between them.

His apartment is the length of an old house, which, from the outside, looks weary, ready to fall to its knees. He lives in the basement, which is only half underground and has very large windows to compensate for the other buried half. She stands in the entrance watching the lower halves of people walking by on their way to church, or to brunch. The opposite wall of the apartment is windowless, brick masked by great boxes of water and light, two immense aquariums. She can't resist walking up to touch the glass, and she watches as the fish dart away from her fingers. The dog follows her up to the glass where he sniffs, looking from the fish to her, as though she can explain. She notices that the dog has tracked in mud from the wet streets outside, his straggly paws wet.

"Oh no. Not on … the man's floor." She realizes in mid sentence that she still does not know this man's name. But this is the strange man's house, with the paw prints tracked across half its length. "Sorry."

He brings a dark blue towel, cleans up the paw prints. She sees the broadness of his back as he stoops to wipe the floor. She sips it in.

"Which one do you like the most?" she asks, gesturing to the tanks of fish. He stands beside her, the edge of his jaw against the smooth line of his neck where she wants to kiss him first.

"The black one there with the semi-circles. He's a Koran Angelfish. There were two others like him, but they died. He's been here the longest. I guess he's just the most familiar."

He realizes he's looking at her, a muscle twitch smile, and he turns back to the tank.

"What's his name?"

"Well, none of them have names."

"And yet you can tell them apart."

"Of course."

"You don't have any blue ones."

He leans towards the tank, noticing this absence for the

first time. "That one's a little blue if you see him up close. You see here, the sand. I put it all level and they've stirred it up into these small hills and valleys. When I first got the tank I put a lot of plants in there. It was a forest, but then they ate them all. I guess they didn't like my ideas."

He leans back from the tank, turns a little to her, then steps back, his hands trying to hide behind him then settling in his pockets. A strange woman he wants to kiss and her dog in his apartment, and he has been talking about fish.

In his nervousness, in the moment of silence immediately following, she sees the door, sees she can leave, can walk back through the rain to the apartment, and nothing will have happened. Nothing. The dog nails click on the hardwood floor over to the door, following her gaze, showing her the exit.

She steps towards the man, then steps even closer when she sees she's caught him with his hands in his pockets and she'll have to make the first move. The first time she's kissed a man and not been kissed first. Her kiss.

They fall asleep after sex. She watches the light from the street wash through the rain, wash through the fish tanks and move on the ceiling, the waltz of seaweed on the ocean bottom. She wakes up with sand in her belly button. Languidly, she runs her hand across her stomach. The two of them deeper down now, full fathoms. He doesn't look like the man from the corner store. That man was a stranger.

They fall asleep and then awake, the lines of the room blurring. They have been here for months now, here in the deep blue.

He tells her the sand comes from the extra blanket he threw on the bed, one he used at the beach, a date with a woman. A date that had not gone well. She felt he had overdone it, Greek salad with mint, roast chicken, pasta with homemade pesto, the wine. Food, he says. She saw it as a sort of pressure. Kate half listens, feels the grit of the sand with her index finger, and imagines she will never leave.

They fall asleep and when she wakes up this time, his back is to her, so she places her chin on his arm and catches a half-glimpse of his face. She sees a flutter of eyelashes, a glimpse of green. His eyes are green, not grey.

"It's my birthday," he whispers into the still of the room, like he's answering the flickering light.

"Happy Birthday."

He brings food balanced in the crook of his arm to the bed, and they watch the light chase the shadows slowly, ever so slowly, yawning across the length of the room. Rice crackers, pâté, sliced avocado, and cheese, maybe Asiago. Bottles of water and a bittersweet juice; he says the name, but she knows she won't remember when she goes looking for it later. They take turns making different combinations of toppings on the crackers. He almost forgets to bring the prosciutto. She watches him eat it with the honeydew melon from which she shucked the seeds with her fingertips. The prosciutto was thinner than any she had had before, and less greasy. She tries eating the two together but has no sense for the taste he bundles into his mouth with a crack of a smile—the sweet and the salty mixed.

She was certain in the moments before she kissed him, before she unbuttoned his shirt, lifted hers over her head in front of an audience of fishes and a dog, that they would be awkward together. It had been years since she had been with any man but Mark. Now, so much later in the day, she runs her hands down his flanks and spreads her thighs a little further apart, almost without thinking. In the bathroom she can hear Riley whimpering softly. She put him there because he was watching her undress, and she found she couldn't cross the room to this Sunday morning man with the dog watching her. He stops whimpering, and she finds herself then absorbed in the quickening pace of this man as he slides between her sweaty thighs, more urgently now. She hears the dog in the bathroom lapping noisily at the toilet water. Sunday man doesn't seem to hear him.

Her eyes open again, the sepia-slanted light washed away, just aquarium light and the chill, bare streetlights through the blinds. She rises from the bed, leaves the man sleeping, moves furtive and quick through the dark, collecting all the discarded pieces, but can't find one sock. He turns over, snuffles, still asleep. She abandons socks. Grabs shoes at the door, her jacket from the back of the chair there, drops keys to the floor. His breathing pauses. She scrambles out the door, her bare feet slapped awake on the slick, naked concrete steps. She jams them into her shoes and ascends the stairs into the drenched Sunday flow, headed for home.

She walks more than a block before she remembers the dog is still in the bathroom. She almost considers leaving him, a casualty of war. As she turns to go back, she sees the man running towards her in a trench coat, with bare feet and the dog on a leash beside him. He smiles and she smiles back awkwardly, for she hadn't planned to see him again unless by accident—and suddenly she finds herself in an accident.

"So you don't want the dog," she says.

"Not really," he says, embarrassed for her. "Listen, um, I'm up and out of the apartment, would you like to go and do something?"

She's nervous, afraid some attachment is forming, and
yet she does not want to go home alone, to wait for a phone
call from Mark.

"Perhaps a movie?" she suggests, realizing that in a
theatre they would not have to talk.

"Yes, a movie would be nice." He has the dog's leash
wrapped around his hand. The dog looks to him for direction and she realizes that she should be holding the leash,
so she takes it from him. "But perhaps we should get you
some shoes or something," she says, noticing the puddle
and his bare feet.

They get shoes from his place. They drop the dog at
hers. She doesn't go in, just lets the dog in, almost pretending it's someone else's house, someone else's home, like she's
dogsitting. She's aware he knows where she lives now, but
tries not to think about it.

She chooses the movie carefully from the theatre marquee
one street over. If it is particularly good they will constantly
be reminded of this night when friends ask if they've seen it.
The scenario could be the same if the movie were particularly bad. The movie has to be mediocre, unmemorable, and
it is—she's chosen carefully. They see a comedy, nothing too
serious.

During the movie his knee touches hers, and in her mind
she pretends they've never met. They are strangers in the
dark, touching for the first time. She only recognizes the
gentle pressure between their knees when his knee gently
relaxes and pulls away.

In the space between them, she feels the tides change.
She believed she was capable of having sex with this man,
of knowing him for no more than an afternoon. And yet here
she is. She should get up from the seat and walk out the door

into the relentless rain. She should go home to the dog, to the phone where she should expect Mark's call.

She finds herself thinking about the fish tanks and the grit of sand in her belly button, the crease between her thighs and groin, behind her ears. The fish, the sand, the gritty sand, the dog whimpering in the bathroom.

She gets up, places one palm on his knee, and as she does she says just one word.

"Sorry." But she says it just as the audience falls into laughter, so he doesn't hear her. At first he assumes she's gone to the washroom, but then she doesn't return. He remembers the touch of her palm on his knee and realizes then that she said goodbye. She's gone, and he can't stay listening to the laughter in the dark theatre, so he goes home, too. A birthday message from his mother, the woman's socks at the foot of the bed, and the Koran fish with his slow, gliding melancholy, missing the other two.

roughhousing

"I have to go," says Dad. "Big sale next week on flank steak. Beef takes up so much room."

Two landslides wiped out the village road last night. Dad is crossing the strait to the city in Tommy Nakasuka's dad's fish boat with some of the other men.

"But the storm's getting worse," mutters Mom from the corner of the kitchen.

"I can swim better than most." He smiles then, his left eye crinkling, almost winking at her.

"Just wish we'd all stay home today. Stormy days, all I want to do is stay in bed. Nestle in. Stay there all day."

"No bed, no roof, if I don't go to work."

I am part of the Formica table, still as steel. We got no school today since the teachers couldn't make it to the village. Scamp fidgets and leg chews in my lap. The worst dog. White poodles don't belong in fishing villages. Too many open sewage ditches and Scamp, she knows every one of them. She prances out the door all white in the morning and staggers back mud-black. But, these days, the government says she has to stay in. She keeps messing up their bear relocation program because she's always jumping into their big cages at the top of the hill by the woods. They threatened to relocate *her* if they come back and find the trap sprung and her inside, chewing on the bait and yapping at them again.

Every morning father leaves for work he throws Scamp out the door, I'm pretty sure so she'll get stuck in those bear traps, and I have to go running after her. She shouldn't be out right now because her belly is beach-balling and Mom keeps saying she's going to burst any day. I pet her lots because I'm the only one who likes her, even with the sewage and burs and getting pregnant. I don't want her to pop so I pet her gently. And now I hide her so Father won't pick her up and throw her out. She'd run right to him. Dogs are like that sometimes, they like the person who is meanest to them the most. She could just splat there on the porch, the way he drops her.

Door slam, Father clunks down the porch steps for the boat.

Mom wails out of habit, "Don't slam ..." and she never finishes.

Quiet floods in and for a second I think it'll be like it's been all week with me sick at home with Mom. Grilled cheese sandwiches, As the World Turns, Mom and me. I think she's happier when Dad is gone.

Mom looks up, marbles on plywood, the rain on the roof. "Where's your brother?"

I don't answer. Just shrug my shoulders. I'm just glad he's gone. I know he's outside, his boots are missing from the front door, and he's probably snuck out by the back door so Mom won't see him go. He's been hanging off my ears all week, see, because I got the chicken pox and he wants them. Mom's been putting that sweet smelling lotion on me, cuddling in behind me on my bed, talking just to me, telling me the story of how we came here, how she and Father showed us a map and let Jake and I choose, our fingers smudging dirt stains and orange pulp across mountains. She let me stay home from school even before the mountain washed out the road, and Jake wants some of all that love. Mom told him to stay away from me or he would get 'em, too, so he hasn't stopped kissing me all week.

Sometimes I figure it might be easier to drown Jake the way Tommy Nagasuka's dad did when their dog had too many of the wrong kind of puppies. Just took them out back in the tortoise tub we played in last summer and held them under where the rainwater had collected. Kept thinking about it when we were in the bath a couple weeks ago.

"Peter, why are you looking at your brother like that? Play nice."

Scared me how she could see what I was thinking. Drowning wouldn't work because Mom would know it was me. So, I figured if I could somehow get him up the hill and into that bear trap they might relocate him to some other family. A bone stupid plan, but I almost got him in the cage when he caught a whiff of the bait, and no bag of marshmallows could ever overpower the reek of that rotting meat. So much for that.

I've only eaten half my cereal, because it's the kind that gets soggy quick. Scamp wriggles in my lap, uncomfortable, but she's making those soft growling purrs because I'm gently petting her bursting belly. Mom's standing at the window looking out over the yard.

"Peter. Where's your brother?"

"Dunno, Mom."

"I mean," and here she takes a deep breath cause she's frustrated and wants me to know it. "I mean, can you go and find him." And this isn't a question.

"Chicken pox."

"You're looking better," she says, her voice hitting concrete.

"Jaaaacooooob!" I holler from where I am sitting.

"Peter!" Mom covers her face with her hands, like she's shutting out every last piece of light. "I could have yelled." She storms over to me and grabs me by the arm. "I meant for you to go and find him. Now put that fat dog down and go and get your brother."

"But Mom—"

"Go get him, mister. Weather's getting worse and I don't want him outside. Bad enough your father crossing the strait in this weather. Look at the colour of that sky. You see the way it's looking at me?"

I'm not sure what Mom's talking about, and not sure if the sky is really looking at her, so I just give her the benefit of the doubt, put Scamp down real careful, back paws, then front paws, and head off to the porch to get my shoes on so I can find that brother of mine. Scamp waddles after me, her belly shoving her legs out from under her, sticking out to the sides like the sawhorses in the gravel yard.

"Stay, Scamp." She can still walk, but the porch steps would be her last fall. I think she senses she will burst soon. Her eyes, goo-encrusted. It's only a matter of time.

The rain falls harder now. Hasn't stopped for weeks, but here and there it falls harder and we stop what we're saying and look up. Or it goes away a little, just fingertips tapping the tin trailer roof. But it doesn't stop. There's more water than air.

Stand in the middle of the yard, just past where Dad parks his old red car. No real yard, not like Tanya Brendalson's, but she doesn't live in a trailer park. No one in our trailer park has grass, like a full lawn. Just patches. Or gravel. Mrs. Neufeldt almost has a lawn, but it's moss and muskeg. And no one goes near her place.

"Jacob!" I holler. "Jacob!" Don't know where to begin looking. I've begun to wonder these last couple of days if he's Satan, that little dark-haired kid in the movie *The Omen*. It was on TV one Sunday. The kid even looked like Jacob. He's like Scamp, see. If there's something he shouldn't be doing, he's perfecting it. So stupid. Like he doesn't even care when Dad comes after him, sleeves half rolled up, biting his bottom lip, his hands clenching ready. Dunno why I care. Dad says if I keep crying every time he hits Jake he's just going to hit me instead. Save time.

"Jacob!"

In that little bitta quiet after I stop screaming Jake's name, I can hear whispers, and I know light-switch where they're coming from. I sneak up to the boards that cover the bottom of the trailer, the boards they put up to try to make the trailer look like a house. The board under the back of the porch comes loose, and that's where you can get at the crawl space. Mom calls it the basement and Dad always snaps back that it's a crawl space, no damn basement. And I can hear whispers in there.

I know there's no quiet way to take this board off, and no matter where he is under there he'll see the daylight come through when I move it. So I got one chance, and one two three I drop the board and it makes this big slamming noise, and I charge in as fast as I can so I can catch him at it.

Problem is I always forget the trailer's on a hill and the space underneath goes shorter and shorter as you go uphill to the back of the trailer, so I go in running and forget it really does become a crawl space by the time you get to the back. About midway to them, me and the beams meet each other and we connect with a real deep thump noise, the kind that sounds like my head splitting open from the root core. I figure I almost knocked the damn trailer off its pilings—Mom must have heard it, too. I'm stunned, real stunned, but my eyes focus quick enough so in the light beaming through from where I tore off the board covering the entrance I can see Jake and Allison trying to get their pants up before I see them. Little twit's dug out his training potty from the storage boxes in the crawl space again, and looks like the two of 'em have been sitting on the old thing. He's five so he's way too old to need a potty and way too young to need it this way.

"What the hell?" I say. "What you doing, Jake?"

"Nothin'," he says. But Allison's only got one leg back in her panties and she falls over, losing her balance trying to get the other one in.

Jake catches me seeing Allison. He scowls at her for giving them away.

"Jake, you put that potty away. Or I'm gonna tell Mom." Guess to some it might not seem a big deal, but see, Allison's my friend Amy's younger sister, and not only that, she's the fourth younger sister I've found him with in one bad way or another in these last two weeks. At this rate I'm gonna run out of friends.

But I don't tell Mom because Jake's always in trouble and he doesn't need any help. And Mom, well, she's cleaning those disks under the stove burners and looks like she might even clean the oven. With the storm and the rain and Father crossing the strait, she's well worried.

When we come back in the house she's sitting at the kitchen table, petting Scamp in her lap. She never does that. Never. Scamp's tongue hangs happily out to the side, but she keeps looking over her shoulder at Mom, like she wonders what gives. Something will give. So I take Jake off to the bathroom to wash his hands. Just like Scamp, he heads outta the house all clean and comes back in after just a few seconds looking like the dirt he's rolled in. Washing his hands is kind of pointless, but Mom will ask him to do it anyway, so I get him to do it before she asks. He looks like he has a tan, even in winter, because the dirt gets into his skin so good it stains him. His face scrunches up when he sees the face cloth and he turns for the hall, but I grab him by the sleeve and tear him back. Takes every muscle, but I lift him up and sit him down on top of the toilet seat.

"Look, Mom's freakin out and just look at her ... she don't need you being a brat. Smarten up. Just be good."

He looks at me squinty, like he's churning out the best way to do the opposite.

"If you're good, I'll let you sleep in my bed tonight. You'll get the chicken pox for sure then."

His little jaw moves back and forth, grinding it over.

"And when the rain stops we'll go outside and you can scream and holler all you want."

When the winter storms shudder-pound the trailer walls. When he has a nightmare. When Mom and Dad make us go to bed early and they yell back and forth in the kitchen. Late at night he'll sneak into my bed, and even though it's too small for even me now, my feet hanging over the end and my neck crinked because my head nudges the head-board, I hang against the edge and hide him between me and the wall. Even if I'm scared too, I feel better pulling the blankets over him and putting my arm around him. I'll say, "It'll be alright," and then I'll believe it, too.

I don't know if Dad hits Mom. My room's too far from the kitchen to hear. She'd never cry, never'd make a noise, and she'd never stop fighting even if he did hit her. Days after the fight she calls Corey's mom and explains it the way she's explained it before. "I'm Irish, he's a mutt," she says. "We're destined to fight."

Jeremy Yamamoto says he's Japanese. I told him I'm an Irish mutt. But I think I'd rather be Japanese.

Mom's sitting at the kitchen table with Scamp still in her lap, and she's doodling on the newspaper. Then the phone rings and scares her so she jumps up and drops Scamp, who yelps on the floor. I grab Scamp, roll her over into my lap, and, gentle like, place my hand on her stomach. Lucky she didn't explode right there on the floor, gizzards everywhere. She whimpers a little as I stroke her belly. I can tell she wants to flip over and she hates lying on her back, but she also wants her tummy rubbed, so she just wriggles around in my lap not knowing what to do.

"Hi Clarice ... no, I haven't heard anything. I'm sure he just went to work as soon as he got there. Yeah. I tried calling, but the phones are out over there. I'll come up after lunch. Talk then. Don't worry. I'm sure he's fine. Bye." It's Mom's the one who's worried, her Scamp petting, the stove half-cleaned, the way she looks up at the ceiling like she thinks it might come down.

She gets up from the chair and moves to the fridge, opens it, and looks. "We should eat," she says. Her voice isn't knotted tight now. Seems telling Clarice not to worry has calmed her down a little, too. For lunch she makes cream salmon on toast and we figure she must be angry with us but we don't know for what. She knows we hate cream salmon on toast. Looks like cat puke. Even Scamp hates it, which just makes it more difficult to get rid of. Last time we had it Jake stuck his plate on the floor and Scamp just took one look at it and puked right there beside it. Sure, she's been sick a lot lately, but that cream salmon on toast didn't help any. Mom came in and saw Jake's plate on the floor and the dog puke and the perfectly good food that she worked so hard to put on the table and provide us with a decent meal even though we're so poor we could be begging for money downtown any day, and she told us once more that we don't know how good we got it. So I was thinking that she always says this and it don't make any sense. We're bloody poorer than the bums down cannery row, but we don't know how good we got it. Makes no sense to me, and all I could think was if I don't know how good I got it, I don't want to know any more than I do. And Jake doesn't know when to quit, as usual, so when Mom picked up the plate and put it back down in front of him he said under his breath,

"Rather eat the dog puke."

And the smack came outta nowhere, so sudden I laughed, scared the laugh right outta me. Jake's eyes went dark as the red came up on his cheek. Problem is he's just like Dad, when you push him he comes back harder than before. Whiplash boomerang. So he started screaming and yelling at her and she just lifted him up with one arm from behind and carried him kicking and hollering down the hall to his room where even the closed door couldn't shut him up.

Today Jake looks at the cream salmon on toast, looks at me like he's doing me a favour, and starts to eat it as quick as he can, holding his breath, gasping for air between swallows. He'd have to be stupid not to see Mom's already on the edge. So we eat as fast as we can, and then we slide down off our chairs. I stack our dishes and put them in the sink, making sure not to bang them. Jacob stands waiting for me between the living room and the kitchen, kind of vibrating because he doesn't know what to do next.

It's raining harder now, and Mom will get angry if we go out, but if we stay in the kitchen she'll for sure find some way to yell at us. So I grab his arm and pull him down the hall to my room. I grab a deck of cards, we climb up on my bed, and we play Go Fish, listening for the rain to stop.

Problem with living in a trailer park is all those trailers are just one big house with thin walls. Everyone in the trailer park knows Jake's a monster, especially since last Christmas when Mr. Kurpil the trailer park owner dressed up as Santa and came around with gifts for all us kids. He'd wrapped up a piece of coal for Jake, just as a joke—I think it was just a big black rock, 'cause there's no coal around here. He had a real gift behind his back waiting for Jake, and I could see it from where I was sitting and unwrapping my present. But you see, Jake figures Santa's really done him in, and you couldn't have blinked your eye from the moment he saw what he'd unwrapped to the moment he threw it against Mr. Kurpil's knee or you would have missed it. But no one missed how Mr. Kurpil fell over backward, crushing Jake's real gift, and no one missed how Jake ended up in his bedroom screaming purple. Dad gave Mr. Kurpil Claus a special drink to go with his cookies, and I got to eat the carrot for the reindeer 'cause Mr. Kurpil Claus said they were retiring this year.

In my room, Jake's throwing half the deck of cards on the floor because he thinks it will be more realistic if we pretend the bed is a wharf and the floor is the water where the fish should be. He does stuff like this all the time when he figures he's losing. Mom comes to the door and tells us it's time for our nap—she usually makes us take one after lunch. Truth told, I never nap. Mom thinks we both do, but with my lights out I hide under my covers and read Archie comics or Nancy Drew mysteries. She's smarter than the Hardy Boys and can do everything they can do but all on her own. Mom says my friend Wendy's mom had to get Wendy glasses because she caught Wendy reading in the dark. So I get to read, don't have to nap, and soon I'll be able to get glasses, just like Wendy.

Mom says she's going up to Corey's mom's place and that the phone is off the hook—if we need her we just yell into the phone. They do this a lot, where they call each other and leave the phone off the hook so they don't have to get all us kids together and don't have to get a babysitter. But I wonder what Mom will do if Dad tries to call and the phone is hooked up to Corey's mom's. Guess it's more important that they visit. Mom hasn't been out of the house all day.

So I read in the dark, today reading Hardy Boys because I am out of Nancy Drew, and I can't remember if I've read this one before but it seems familiar, the haunted house on the cliff, the secret case file their dad is working on. I never get to finish them because when Jake's angry at me he sneaks into my room and dumps everything in my room on the floor, and the bookmarks get lost in the jumble. I hid the books beneath the mattress for a while, but I think he felt them one night when he slept in my bed. Like that fairytale with the princess and the pea, or like the time on *Sesame Street* when Cookie Monster was the princess and they put a cookie under the mattress. Jake and the Hardy Boys.

With Jake asleep in the next room and Mom going up the hill to Corey's mom's, I can hear the rain on the roof now, pebbles pouring on metal. I look up at the ceiling, wonder if it won't just wash us all into the ocean. It's possible. I wonder if the boat capsized. If Dad is drowning. If he's dead. I think about how we'll survive without him.

Maybe we'll end up down by the docks scavenging with the bums. Or maybe we'll move to the city and beg for money on the streets. Or maybe Mom will meet a rich guy and we'll live in a bigger city and we'll get lots of *Star Wars* toys for Christmas instead of new gumboots. Maybe. Or maybe he'll come home.

Once, when Mom was up the hill at Corey's, I put on thick socks and soft-shuffled over to the phone where it was lying off the hook on the table. I listened to our two moms, and I can't say I heard even one word, but I heard them laugh, laugh like they didn't when we were there, telling stories they didn't tell when we were around.

Today I move, breath held, into Mom and Dad's room. I climb on the tangled, unmade sheets and blankets and look up at the ceiling, listening to the rainfall on the roof there. Sounds louder there for some reason, don't know why. I turn my head. Mom's side of the bed smells like Mom in the morning, soap and flannel and garlic. The phone is on her bedside table, so I pick it up and listen to see if I can hear her talking on the other end. I sit down on the floor beside the bed, and the shag carpet tickles the backs of my legs. There's no laughing, just hushed voices and I can't tell which one's Mom's. And from where I sit I can see on the wall above Mom's closet how a brown stain from water leaks is spreading across the white wall, and it looks like the colour of the old photos of Grandma and Grandpa and other people I don't know.

Suddenly there are no voices on the other end. Rain rat-a-tatting heavier. And then I realize it's because the phone is dead. Like thunder rumbles, the sound of raindrops on the roof, because there's no other noise. Then I hear thumping up the front steps so I hang up the phone and run back to my room and jump beneath the blankets. I'm sure it's Mom. I hear the floor creak in the usual places, quiet so she won't wake us. She stops just outside my door and I can hear her peek through the crack where it's open a bit.

"Peter," she whispers. "Are you reading in the dark again?"

I don't answer. I don't think she's angry with me, I think she's just lonely. Probably wants someone else to be awake in the trailer, in the rain. And then her footsteps move down the hall to their room, and I stay quiet under the covers, waiting, thinking I might read, but I fall asleep.

— — —

Last light leaking through the rain on the window, bang of lids on pots in the kitchen. This is the worst time of day, with the light going away and the day all finished except dinner. Worst 'cause Dad's coming home and Jake's waking up, and he never wakes up in a good mood.

I hear my door creak open. It's Corey, pig-tailed with chained-dog eyes, a doll strangled in her left hand, and she's looking at me but I don't know why.

"What you doing here?"

"My mom brought us down. We're staying here tonight."

"You're lying."

"No way. Just ask your mom."

I get up out of bed and push past her and down the hall. Sometimes Corey's my best friend. Sometimes I just have to play with her because she has the biggest yard.

"Mom!" I yell as I come around the corner into the kitchen. She looks up from the kitchen table where she's sitting with Corey's mom, and they're not cooking dinner and they don't speak. They return to staring at the middle of the kitchen floor. Corey's mom's sour, thin lips clench up

when she's angry, and they do now, but she doesn't seem
angry when she says to me, "Peter, go wake up your brother
and then all you kids go play quietly in the living room."
I turn and walk from the kitchen and down the hall to
Jake's room. But I don't wake him up, I just climb under
the covers with him and he grumbles a little, but I just tell
him "It's okay," and I can tell by his breathing he's fallen
back asleep. Corey and her sister can play by themselves.

A little later I can hear banging in the kitchen and it
sounds like someone's cooking, so I shake Jake awake.

"Hey."

"What!" Jaw tense, hunched, still half asleep, half growling in a leg trap.

"No. Don't be grumpy. Corey and her mom and sister
are staying with us tonight."

"What?"

"I mean, I need you to be good. For me." He opens his
eyes wider, looks right at me. He nods, yawns, and rubs
the side of his head where the hair is all splayed.

In the kitchen, Corey's mom cooks dinner.

"Welcome back to the land of the living," she says, but
she doesn't seem happy we've come back. She always says
stuff like this and she hardly ever seems happy. Corey's dad
left her a while back, before we came to the village.

She's making cream salmon on toast. I turn around and
see Jake's face scrunching up like he's about to say something and so I flare him a warning look and tell him to go
off to the living room. He says nothing, but he stomps his
feet a little as he crosses to the living room where Corey
and her sister are playing.

"Where's my mom?" I ask her.

"She's just put her head down to have a nap." She turns

to me and then kneels down on the floor so her face swallows mine. "She's a little worried because your father never phoned and now the phone lines are out in the village. She's just nervous. We're going to stay down here with you guys to keep you company and," as she straightens up to stir the cream salmon, "we'll have an overnight party, a slumber party. We'll all sleep in the living room and we'll make 'smores." She's acting cheery now, and coming from Corey's mom this is like when a badger shows you his teeth—there's no way to believe it's a smile.

In the living room Jake sits on the couch, arms crossed, glaring at Corey and her sister marching their dolls around on the floor, telling doll stories in little screechy voices. Two of the four dolls are missing heads and one is completely naked. Corey looks up at me as I come into the room.

"I think your dad's dead."

I look at Jake and he gets up and kicks her in the leg and sits back down.

"Hey! Jerk!" she says, and her face flashes into a fist, like she's going to really start crying, and I can hear her mom behind us clanging the spoon against the edge of the pot, stirring the cream salmon, and I'm figuring the only thing worse than getting our mom mad is getting Corey's mom mad. So I sit down beside Corey and put my hand on her shin where Jake kicked her.

"Jake's sorry. We're just worried. How about we all play dolls or something," I say.

Her face unclenches, still red in splotches, her eyes grim with a smile.

"We'll play orphanage," she says.

Then the room goes black, silent. No lights outside either. Relief just to hear the rain pouring down on us.

We all sit for a second, everything erased, until Corey's mom says from the kitchen,

"Damn it. I can't finish cooking.... Now what are we going to eat?"

And I can hear Jake smiling clear across the room.

— — —

We all sleep in the living room, not for fun, but because without the power there's no heat and a trailer with a fireplace ain't never been made or we've never seen it. We have cheese and crackers and celery sticks for dinner. Anything's better than cream salmon on toast. Jake and I aren't as tired as the others, and Mom can't sleep, so we sit on one side and she whispers stories to us so that we won't fidget too much and wake up the rest.

"...and then they added another mattress to the pile and they waited to see if she could feel the cookie underneath all that. She didn't sleep well that night so they knew she was a princess."

She's telling us the *Sesame Street* version, the one with Cookie Monster as the princess.

"But wouldn't the cookie have crumbled?" I ask.

"Well, it was one of those chewy, bendy kinds...."

"Not like Grandma Pearl's. They're like rocks," says Jake. Mom doesn't say anything to this. I think I can see her smile.

"Time we try to sleep," she says to us. Jake's eyes are only half open now. She lies down on her back and pulls us in on either side of her so our heads lie in the crooks of her arms. Scamp lies down beside me.

I don't wake up until the sun is up, blaring through the gauze curtains Mom decorated all the living room windows with. At first I can't remember my dream. We hear footsteps on the stairs then see Dad on the porch. He smiles through the window as he opens the door. I roll over and burrow my head in Mom's armpit, but she lets go of me as she sits up and then lurches towards Dad. Jake's eyes holding mine fist-grip. I know we are both remembering our dreams from last night. Boats sinking, and water, all the water sweeping overhead and fishes pulling down and some even kissing goodbye, and we could see from the shore that the rain felt different, because it was dream rain. And it wasn't a bad dream. Wasn't a bad dream at all.

freighters

Six freighters anchored in the bay today. All facing south.
The sky gasps open and the rain falls askew, almost absent
minded, keeps falling while the sunlight slicks and shatters
off the shop windows, the concrete towers, the world on
the edge of melt.

On the bus, you tell me how you fall in love with bus
drivers, their hands. A list of fragments you desire, then
you confess that a poem you gave me is about my lips. My
lover's hands, too. I confess to you that my lover's hands
seem like paws, like in *Gorillas in the Mist*. Wise hands.

You and your lover have opened your relationship.
For the length of the bus ride, you use manifesto words:
experimental, counter-culture, radical, anti-oppressive.

After the bus, the hands, you stop outside the Vogue
Theatre and are suddenly entranced by the sidewalk, the
montage of clear glass blocks embedded out front. And
while you are looking down, I look up, across the street,
and I point out to you what I see: through steamed-up
windows, glazed, the silhouettes of ballet dancers stretch
and spin in the third-storey window. And we both stand
in the rain and cannot move because it smells of grace,
random and ripe and taut all at once.

I tell you that my lover and I are trying to keep a closed
relationship. That with so many gay couples arguing for

"openness" and "liberation," it seems radical to stay monog-
amous. And I wonder, I ask you, why you get to use words
like "open" and I am left with words like "closed."

We are going to buy de Sade's *Justine*, a copy for each of
us, because we are both going to read it. A form of flirting.

— — —

The day after we buy the *Justines*, we are walking along the
bay. I ask that we walk on the sand, because my lover has
told me not to. It's his job to sweep the apartment and he
hates it when I track in sand. Out on the bay, eight freighters face north. I tell you that what I miss most about being
single are the threesomes, touristing in their beds, mapped
with hands and ardour, keys and shoes waiting at the door.

Then the wind changes, suddenly blows from the mountains, not the water, and brings thunder and those tropical
showers. All the queeny boys who have done their hair just
right and haven't brought their new raincoats have to laugh
off their disarray, shaking off and scattering raindrops on
the coffee house floor. Cavalier, almost butch. Necessity is
the butch of invention.

At our table, looking out at the rain, I want to ask you to
dance, shunt my chin against your neck, a close waltz saying
it'll be all right. "It" being that we're in relationships where
we ordered a chocolate shake at the drive-thru window, but
the woman keeps saying through the speaker, "onion rings,"
and we repeat, "choc-o-late," and she repeats, "onion rings,"
and there's only one road out of there and she only has
onion rings and we don't feel heard. Analogies are always
disappointing.

And sometimes when we read to flirt, I want to read you,
pour a cup of tea, hold you in both hands, with good light,
and I won't even mind when my coda mind slips away and

back, reading the same line, "a fragment of you held against the roof of my mouth to ward off," then "a fragment of you held," over and over, "a fragment." A type of lingering, the repetition of you. And I might undress the text, hold your parchment up to the light when no one is looking.

The next morning, only three ships. Never seen so few. In the afternoon I watch you at the gym and watch you furious with your body, remaking it, me and the shrinking others, caught in the mirrors on all sides, watching. I leave the gym thinking about your fidget fingers in the café the night before, the way you fingered the pages then turned them, brusque and final.

Later you tell me how that man at the gym with the chewed, ragged fingers and thin mouth took you home and dragged teeth up your ribs, punctuation bruises, how you staggered home in the rain, the city rife with looks and accusations.

The city—towers with looks now, windows turn to face you, misreading the muscles ridged along your lateral plane, torqued and tantalus. You start to chew your fingers through your smile, thinning.

And I feel tupperwared compared to you. And I wonder if that's true. Why "closed," not "open"?

I told you once how I feel drawn to the freighters in the harbour, how they turn, synchronized swimmers, with the tide changes, all facing south, all facing north, all with their backs to us as though to leave, but hunkered back, still anchored. Suspended in motion.

My lover is afraid that if he left me I would go to you, and I'm afraid that if I keep grinding my teeth at night they will shatter. The worst thing in the world, to be here without a grin to bear it.

Yet, somewhere between the tides, the water in uncertain eddies, time hangs. No measurements for the generic days, an accidental taste I found. Days that matter because they resemble the others. There are no pictures of these times.

And you wrote a poem about my lover's hands, the strength of them, thick beasts, you said. And I wonder how you separate that from how he hit me that night, backhanded. It wasn't his stupidity that bothered me, not the suddenly articulate well of his angry marrow, but the appearance of it, who it irrevocably made me, in the hours of the next morning between the mirrors. And I want to call my mother and say, "I am the woman you never let yourself become," for she kicked my father out before he could hit her, though sometimes words leave larger marks.

Maybe it's best that we got that backhand out of the way, and context is everything—amber rum, old lover, thicker hands, deep-veined thirst—but I wonder if I flinch more than usual, or whether I will ever admit what I really thought when the back of his fist connected. That this connect, this impact, was a relief, and all I could think was, "There, now that's out of the way."

In the café, I watch you read, my copy open in front of me. I remember when I was a kid and my parents would be having one of their shred-the-linoleum and ricochet fights, how my brother would sneak into my bed, shivering, not crying, and how I would hold him and tell him, "It'll be all right," and how telling him almost made me believe it. I search my mind for something to tell you now, something I might believe. I watch you turn the page.

thirst

What holds the village to itself. The industry along the
docks, the cannery row, the learning in the plank-flat
school, the quiet circles of eagles flying over the houses in
wider arcs, and then back to the garbage dump. Shit hawks.

— — —

Memory shapes differently here. In green muddled to dark
root, fronds sprung from muskeg floor, reaching to bare,
discarded light. In the pulpy core mulch of bones, dampness
ripples. The real scar's inside, runs skeletal, root ache for the
lack of rain. A dry season, so long without rain, would leave
us not enough water to see straight. Days shale brittle so we

might just collapse in on ourselves, the muskeg scarecrows. Can't see how thirsty we are until you take away the wet. Echoes of our thirst vibrato where we thought bones lay. Then the mountains would sinkhole, the ocean recoil in disgust at lips licked ragged, no longer caring about the salt, no longer, just sidling up to that body of salt water, licking. Words would fall off the trees half formed, only letters so the cannery row mongrels collect them together and make up their own language, and every second word will be another word for water.

=====

Butchering, like any trade, requires special tools. The carpenter refines his skill with each tool. So, too, the butcher. Particularly when cutting beef it is necessary to have several tools to do the job properly. Necessity begs for invention, though, so if you do not have access to a meat saw just use a carpenter's saw ... A craftsman needs his tools. People respect a man who takes his craft seriously.

So hot this summer. Mom made iced tea everyday and she said to Aunt Lizzy, "Can't see how thirsty you are until you take away the wet. Then you can hear the whispers, and there's thirst where you thought you had bones." Lizzy said Mom's a damn poet. No rain all summer until that first day of August, the hottest day of that summer when all the adults were sleeping, and we could only play in the shade of the trees, slow games. That's when Tony said it started. Middle of that sweat-stained afternoon, he was doing the constable's wife like a dog, because she liked it that way and that's how she'd taught him to do it. Tony said so. Tony's only twelve, alder thin, but his nads grew in early, earlier than the rest of him. He is a boy with a man's parts.

Bigger than most men, he tells us. Tony said that he was ramming her, the constable's wife, when he heard her start to cry and that she put her hand to her head like this and then her body began to shake and he thought she was just going to do what she normally did. But then the flames ran up her spine. Then she threw her head back and screamed, reached round and ripped off both his balls.

He didn't tell us the rest of the story because he was bleeding there on the constable's bed, though I could see he still had both his balls. Tony tells big stories. Still, there was blood.

But we didn't need to hear the story from him because we were the kids under the big pine tree in her front yard, playing when she came stumbling down her front steps with her one arm reaching in the air, the other raking at her breasts, and all that blood running down towards her armpit. Her arm shook, a fish gasping in bare air, and then she wailed again, but then it changed so it was a groan, the sound of mooring lines straining on the ships when they shift in the tide. Windows up and down the streets shattered then, as the walls of trailers on trailer row crumpled in like empty pop cans, and the houses caught domino fire on down to the water. The chipboard shacks where the fishmongers lived fell flat to the ground, and then streets filled up with all our parents moaning that same long moan. And we followed, close at first, crying. Mom and Aunty Lizzy had shards from their iced tea glasses stuck in their open palms as they staggered into the mass of adults moving towards the water.

We thought it was the heat, the thirst. Old fishermen and the net menders and the cannery line hags all staggered into the streets, all shook and walked out to the breakwater, out into the harbour. There must have been a small breeze off the water because the smell of them soon reached back to shore, like sulfur, like fire, and we the children stood on the beach trying to outcry each other, pointing at the crowd of adults out on the jetty, "my mother," "my sister," "my mother's friend," everyone we were losing. The stink of them tried to drive us off the beach, where the older kids showed the younger ones how to hold rotting fish carcasses to their noses, like the soldiers did in the war with rags soaked with their own urine, like Mrs. Neufeld had told us, her left hand cupped and held in front of her face in front of the class, the only way to escape poison gas. And we held the carcasses to our faces among the broken shells, pebbles, and torn scabs of seaweed, and we breathed.

At the edge of the dock, then, I could see my father, his white apron pockmarked with bloodstains. I could see from here. A butcher in a fishing village isn't very useful, my mother always says. Still, he was training my hands to be like his. He would hold them out, the big fingers, scarred and animal thick. And he'd get me to place mine on top, delicate in comparison. He thought I'd grow up to be a butcher, too. Out there on the dock, his arms in the air, wailing with the others, he was not my father.

The stench of their thirst congealed around their feet on that point, the thick yellow of jaundice. And one of the empty fishermen, the one who survived the war with a plate in his head, pummelled his head with his hands, as if to move around the water left in him, beat the flesh raw, until we could see the plate glinting in the roaring sun. He beat the plate until his metal watch sparked against it. The thirst fog took quick fire, and the flames shot out in tendrils, an octopus' garden of fire spreading towards us.

A sudden root-pain thirst shuddered us on the shore, so we ran through the lickings of the barnacles, skirted the village fires, and climbed the mountain away from the screams of the adults on the dock, the spreading flames.

Those of us who made it far enough up the mountain looked back down on the red rash fire, the crackling, collapsing trailers and shacks. Then there were those of us who delayed, like Caroline from the fourth grade, chasing her tail-less cat among the burning shacks, the smoke cindering her lungs, her eyes bulging, her skirt then a burst of light, a match catching. Like that, just like that, the word *home* was gone.

Thirst fevering us, we dug down in the muskeg with our bare fingers to find the water table, and even though we could not see how we would get out of the forty-foot holes we'd dug, we didn't care. We ate handfuls of muskeg full up with wood bugs and lice looking for the same thing as us. And we slept in the pits for four nights and dreamed that dew would collect in our eye sockets, that we would wake underwater, 'til we blinked it all away, just an open-eyed dream.

Days later, when we found our way out from the pits, we saw the singed pile of bodies through the trees, the point out on the breakwater where a fish and chip shop used to stand, the bodies still burning, unquenchable, and they'd been burning before, and even a miracle couldn't stop the fire. All the boats in the bay caught fire while we'd been away, and those that hadn't sunk under to lay in comas on kelp beds that were smouldering now, carcasses tossed against anchor chains.

No more adults, just a village full of children and memories of rain jackets and umbrellas.

The mountains are happy now, don't want the rain to return. We've had rains so strong in the past they've wiped the mountains faceless. Even the mountains are still scarred, paler green trees growing where the rain washed away the land.

We are so alone here now, no roads out from this island village. Don't know whether to pray for rain, or for adults, or both. And the smoke from the burnt bodies, the burnt canneries and boats, make scorched, smoky sunsets for days and days after.

=

Always make sure the knives are sharp and prepared for the slaughter. The easiest way to control the blade while you sharpen it is to place it in a vice or frame made of wooden molding on a work bench. When using a stone make sure you sharpen the blade at a fifteen to twenty degree angle. Sharpen your knives well away from the barn so you won't scare the animals.

We grow younger each day. We forget.

We play. Race everywhere. Skip. Climb trees, the mountains behind the village, one another stacked into pyramids. Throw rocks out along the rolling bay or at each other. We play because we don't want to grow old before the rains return, before we age into the fire that took our parents, the other adults. When the younger ones cry at night because we are all so alone, we do not tell them fairy tales, we make shows with our hands against the stars, about children racing up trees, throwing rocks at other children, shows where nothing happens but one thing after another. For to tell a story is to grow old, but to make it, act it out, is to play, to be a child.

Thirst not sheet-flash lightning now, just dull toothache. Berries slake away slivers of it. The juice of bugs, handfuls of moss deeper down near where the pond was, blood from squirrels and small animals when we can snare them. But the little ones will only eat berries. And we don't work too much, take turns collecting berries and make sure we play extra hard after workdays, and sometimes make the work a game, the child who gathers the most handfuls getting to be leader for a day. We've mended the nets, and if we play in the shallows and run we can catch smaller fish. There are no boats to trawl the deeper waters, and no need, really, because we can catch the smaller fish in the shallows.

There are no fish boats or fishermen anymore, so the harbour boils with sea lions and, because there are so many sea lions, soon there are more orcas than we have ever seen, so only the older kids have the courage to go anywhere near the ocean.

Some days, though, the hottest days, we all play in the water at Cassiar Beach, where the old cannery once stood. It burnt down long before this dry season, before the fire, so we find old bits of glass well worn by the sea, and we pretend they are gems. Corey takes it too far, holds them to her fingers like rings and to her ears like earrings, talks of everything she will buy, how rich she will be. Then she glimpses the younger ones watching her, faces scrunched in confusion, and catches herself. We don't talk about the future.

We must keep on playing, even though it means we get hungrier. Play harder, work harder, and both are good because they both make us sleep better, and the nightmares will only come to the oldest of us. We have more nightmares because the younger ones barely remember what we work each day to forget.

The youngest children have begun the forgetting, sometimes forget they ever had parents. All they know is this mountainside and the paths down to the ocean, the crag gully, the bare, empty riverbed, the taste of muskeg, and water beetles that have never known open water. I wonder what it must be like to be free from the alphabet, to know only the sounds taught to you by the wind, the ocean water, a palm pile of glass gems.

Shanks curdled blue and black with poisoned sap, the faded brown of the evergreens. What I won't tell the others is this: the slow-fire burn in my crotch, the cords of my legs. I am slowly becoming an adult, I know this. But I don't want to let go, don't want to break the circle of play and work, and even if I did, what then? Should I walk to the water's edge and wait for the flames to itch up from under my skin 'til I dance there with the licking? The flesh has a mind of its own, and if I could cut it away I would. I see the glint of fire in the others' eyes, the ones the same age as me. Sometimes we look at each other sideways, seeing what we won't admit. But then they run ahead, or bend down to play with the smaller ones. We start to avoid each other. I wonder if it's not stronger in me. Catches me up. Like this morning when the runner, the biggest of those boys my age, got a bleeding nose, and one of the other boys tipped his head back. I knew the blood would flow down his throat, that he should lean forward, but I could only watch. Could see the throb of pulse in his neck, thrown back. The desire to stop the pulsing rivulet just under the skin of his neck. The thought that I could not admit to anyone, and the fire that burned it into my flesh, thickening musculature.

Above all, when killing the animal, make sure that you don't scare them. Kindness is the key, for if the animal is scared and adrenalin is released into the meat it will spoil. However you kill the animal, make sure the heart continues to beat briefly after the slaughter so that the animal can be properly bled.

You'll want to butcher on cool days, but not when night temperatures will fall past freezing so watch the weather forecasts when you are planning to butcher.

And it's sunset now, and it's us older kids that feel our bodies yearning towards the west, the water line, and we know it's like sleepwalking and that we'll not wake up until we're there with the flames, and we will become what we've always been. This long, long wordless scream from the gut.

We think we know what will happen, yet it hasn't happened to any of us yet. Only that one day, when all the adults caught fire. I catch Cara and Siever looking at the horizon, and they look back to gathering berries or playing marbles with the smaller ones. I think we all secretly yearn for the rains, hope they might come before then. I fear there will never be any rains, that maybe there never were any. When the others aren't looking, I shove bleeding handfuls of berries into my beast mouth, snuffling and licking as I take more than my share.

On the way to find more berries, we find a deer, guts split open, blistering with the dryness, flies humming over every last bit. I see the sinews, can see the joint of the deer's hip where a blade could easily cut the limb from the torso. My father once showed me this in the garage with a moose, the vulnerable places where limbs meet bodies and a well-sharpened blade can divide the two. "Feel your way," he said, his hand running into the groin of the dead animal. I remember this, the blood pooling on the garage floor, the smell, the half-rot beast smell of something wild. I look up from the splayed deer on the path and see Cara watching me. We look away and keep walking.

Fewer berries each day, less juice so less water. We are rotting through with dryness. Dry rot. Brittle. Nothing left to absorb the rains if they did come.

And most of the birds flew off long ago. Only the ones who catch their own fish stay, for the fishes' bodies filter out the salt, cradle moisture. These birds have to eat more fish to get this moisture, though, and we watch them hunting the streams all day long, but the streams are drying into trickles now that the snowcaps have melted entirely, a coast of naked mountains.

And the squirrels burrowed down through the dry muskeg, live underground like groundhogs or moles, snuffling out the moisture that escapes us, in underground streams. There aren't many more animals.

A trip up the hill to search for berry patches further up, wolves prowl in the treeline, teeth bared in a grimace so they can barely see over their mouths. A few days ago, down at the beach, one of them prowled right out of the woods and grabbed one of the smaller kids by the ass. The kid was just dabbling in the shallows when the wolf bolted out of the treeline and bit him. The wolves act alone now, have abandoned their packs, desperate enough to abandon each other but at a loss to know how to hunt alone, they resort to stupid attempts like this. Siever came running and I grabbed a piece of driftwood and beat the wolf off the kid while Siever threw stones. The wolf ran for the trees, then lurked back out, skulked down the beach towards another kid, and we had to chase him back into the trees again. We did that three or four times. I thought he'd just keep trying until we killed him. I thought about killing him. We could use the meat. Then he didn't come back.

That wolf's been following us off and on for days now, so I almost feel sorry for him. One of us has to fall to him soon. He's waiting for that moment. With fewer berries and the streams almost gone, we can't support the twenty-three kids we have. We've had to take to working a lot more than playing to survive. And those of us that are older are certain this means the fire will come sooner than planned for us. We'll grow old before it's our time.

═══

Cut the animal's throat as soon as you've killed it, a long clean cut just behind the jaw and as deep as you can go. You will be able to tell you've cut the necessary veins when you see and hear the blood gushing.

Remove the skin from the inside out to avoid leaving pieces of hair attached to the meat, and let gravity help you by removing the skin as you hoist the carcass up.

One of the smaller kids, Peter, the one with red hair, tells us he's allergic to fish and shellfish. We've had to double our efforts, working in the bay and taking risks by sending kids up into the woods to find more berries and plants he can eat. Of Cara and Siever and I, I'm the biggest, so I'm usually the one to take the red-headed kid into the woods to get berries. He won't eat muskeg. The bugs. Yesterday and today we saw another wolf. This one's different, hangs back, doesn't lurch forward desperately, but my gut falls when I see it watching Peter. The wolf knows Peter is weak.

Our little red-headed kid. If we send him into the woods alone he'll be killed. We're really just delaying what will happen anyway.

I feel sorry for the wolf, because he's just like us: so, so hungry. It occurs to me that if I let the wolf get this kid, I might be securing the survival of our group for a little while longer, keeping the strong alive. We won't have to work so hard, and maybe that will give those of us closer to the fire time ... time to wait for the rains, time to figure out some way to keep from burning.

I think it's hunger, these little pangs, but then they rise up to my throat, a spurt of bile, as I look at that gentle, white, delicate neck. What I am thinking makes me sick. I watch Peter's milk pudding softness as he idly picks berries and then watches a bird fly slowly overhead. I try talking to the kid. Peter. But he just whines about how he hates berries and plants, talks about the grilled cheese sandwiches and pickles his mom used to feed him, but I think he makes it all up because none of us remember that far back. He calls himself Peter. I almost laugh, 'cause it's like that story my mom once read to me. Peter and the wolf. Maybe it's a sign. Maybe I'm the one who's supposed to make it happen. I figure the way to make this happen is to let the other kids think that me and Peter have become best friends, then I'll always be the one to help him forage for food, and then when the wolf attacks on some routine food hunt I will cry, and I will have lost a friend. They'll never know. I wonder if I'll do it.

— — —

We just got back from a trip to the trees where we found something terrible. We found the old wolf, the one that bit the kid by the beach a few days ago. At least I think it's him. His friends, the other wolves, had eaten everything off him, his bones scattered across the clearing. Through the neck we could almost see up inside his skull where the bugs were eating—it was smouldering in there. That's all we saw, though, because then Peter threw up and fainted. Wasted all the berries we had collected so far, so I was almost going to make him eat his own puke. Perfectly good waste of food. It's harder and harder to find berries. No more leaves on the trees. Even the evergreens have lost all their needles.

Noon the next day, we hear crackling and a whoosh, look up the hill from where we're picking berries and see a tree gulped by fire in minutes, crumbling to the ground. Then another, clear across the meadow, bursts into flames, too, snowing black ashes down around us. Siever and me start pushing the kids to rush down the hill. One by one the trees combust behind us. We call to Cara, grab the berries we've saved, the blanket we found by the beach, but we don't have much time. We get the rest of the group to the beach. We sit on the driftwood watching the trees burn each other down. Soon there will be nothing, just ocean and rocks.

I caught one of the smaller kids smashing barnacles and eating them today. They don't taste great, and there's not much to them, but the kid showed us what we've been missing. There's more than fish in the ocean. Cara discovered that two of the eight-year-olds can hold their breath the longest, have bigger lungs, so they've become our official divers, going down for all kinds of shellfish and a few experimental things like urchins or sea cucumbers. Cara and Siever always keep lookout on shore in case the orcas come into the shallows, hunting after the divers.

Using the length of the backbone as a guide, saw the carcass into two equal halves, leaving only a few inches of neck tissue to hold the halves together. When quartering the carcass, keep a few inches of flank attached to hold the quarters together when you cut across the backbone. Cut between the last two ribs on each side. Most butchers display charts to help pinpoint where.

Peter's not just allergic to fish and shellfish, he sneezes all the time. I think he's allergic to dirt and trees and maybe air. There's always a line of snot flowing out of his nose and I have a hard time looking at him. Sometimes he just sits down and cries, something about his mother. On our trips looking for berries and leaves it's mostly me that does the looking and he just cries or pokes around with a stick. I have to keep reminding myself that he's just a kid.

I know it's probably not right, but when I look at Peter all I can think about is how easy it would be to grab his head with both hands and tilt it suddenly to snap his neck. And then he'd stop jabbering about all the G.I. Joes and Pokémons he used to have. When we're with the group I watch him and I notice the other kids push him down and he cries, or they try to run away so they can skip rocks or play castle without him, and he follows them crying. He's just a pain in the ass.

I think I would be doing the group a favour. I think the other kids will see that.

— — —

Saw the other wolf again today and he took up our trail, followed us from camp to ocean and back. If I turn my back on him, he comes closer, low to the ground, teeth bare, so

I know if I don't make my move soon this one will die just like the old one and I'll run out of ways to get rid of Peter. Can't have a Peter without the wolf. Well maybe you can, I can't really remember how the story goes. But I'll have to move soon because I can smell the smouldering on this wolf already.

I think the wolves miss their packs. While the others sleep, I stand and walk down the beach a little, find Siever sitting on a log. We listen to the trees, some still burning, crackling in the dark. We say nothing. The wolves' cries echo off the mountainside as they call to each other, the ones who are still alive, missing the others of the pack. Maybe they are wondering if it isn't better to starve together, as a pack rather than alone.

One of the smaller children started telling the other kids that when you hear your stomach growl, it's the sound of your stomach eating you, hollowing out your insides. It wasn't until one of the girls started crying that we explained to them that it was a lie. But now I wonder. I think the fire works that way. Burns this space inside of you 'til it burns right through your skin, leaps into the air and catches flame where it can finally breathe. I can feel it tickling just below my skin. There isn't much time.

For Peter's berries today, we have to head further north up the coast. We run across three wolves, one after the other, not hunting together, desperately following us just inside the treeline, no cover but the burnt remains of trees. Two start ripping into each other, fighting over who saw us first maybe, and the third takes this as a sign to lunge closer to us. So we have to run to get back to the group, me dragging Peter blubbering along the stones and drift-wood beach. If I don't kill him the wolves will. They smell what I smell on him, that sour milk weakness, the pulpy give of his flesh when I grab his arm. Maybe the fire in me is the hunger changing my body. I will know what it means when I suddenly break open, letting out the howl.

═══

The secret to meat lasting is clean hands. It is also the secret to good tasting meat. A good butcher takes cleanliness seriously.

The thunderheads have moved in from the ocean; we are certain to get rain. Off the coast the thunder has begun to rumble and the wolves have gathered on the ridge above the camp. They have rejoined their packs and they howl along with it. The smouldering in me burns a little hotter, waiting for the rain. I think the rain might quench this, might save Peter's life.

A flash and the bay ripples where the rain hits it, corrugates the smooth water, sheets of rain washing over the bay towards the shore. Our mouths are open and our faces are dry bone. The rains have come and a grim and raw clenching comes with them, not relief.

With the sound of the rain pattering sand we all begin to jump in the air, and we are ripping off what clothes we have and throwing ourselves in the ocean, stamping in the puddles that instantly form 'cause the earth can't swallow it fast enough. Before we know it the killer whales have pushed their way up onto the shallows and ripped away two of the smallest of us, flailing. The shallows are red and torn with bubbles, and yet the horrible thing is we hardly notice. Those of us in the water move to the shore and writhe on the beach in the falling rain, and it hurts, the rain drops are the biggest I have ever seen and they smack our naked skin.

We're naked, and I know I will have no other chance but this with all the kids caught in the sheets of rain, the grip of the thirst swallowing us in so much water, so I grab Peter and throw him over my shoulder and run up the beach to the treeline, slipping on slick stones. At the lip of the ravine, I throw him over the edge and leap after. We're on the downward slope to the dry riverbed now, where the others won't hear. Lost in the rain, I doubt they can anyway. And he's naked, his flesh milk pudding and soft under my hands as I grab his neck and he fights to break free on the muddy slope of the ravine. Only then do I realize he's been screaming. Because it's just a gasping now. My hands have muffled it. He is soft everywhere, and even my father wouldn't know where to begin to cut.

The slope slides off itself, relief and loss. I lose my balance, but my hands dig into Peter's fleshiness and pull him with me as we slip down the embankment. Sliding down the slope, dirt soaks up gushes of water, ripples into mud, more waves of mud, slides down the hill, a stream, then a river of mud. I flip onto my back, pulling him over onto my chest, my hands crushing around his pulpy neck, and he's writhing around but if he's screaming I can't hear him because of the thunder, because of the rumble of the mud washing off the mountains and off the ravine and flowing down. In this moment in the flood I begin to laugh, and I am crying, too, this laughter from my belly, my hands tight around his neck, holding us together. We are mud and water.

Rains flood through the trees, swell into a river, mud and water, and I have to push my head to the surface to breathe and then I am under laughing, waves of bubbles, and Peter has stopped squirming, but I'm laughing so hard I can't tell. We crash through a wave of bubbles, where the river washes into the bay. We are floating, out on the ocean where it is calmer now. Without the flow of the river to buoy us we sink a little, my hands letting go. The cold saltwater bubbles in where my hands and his flesh were scorched together, burned from the grip. Air a thick grey slate, the crisp hiss of the rain along the flat water of the bay, I tread water, but Peter sinks under, not moving, not swimming.

I feel them first like a shadow, a gap in the silence. The killer whales, rubbing their black rubber skin up against us. They call out to one another. They say sailors thrown overboard can drown when they hear whales calling out to one another, that the calls can make humans laugh so hard, tickle them down in their diaphragms until they drown. In the sea of squeals and water, curling and shifting under, I suddenly feel a sadness. I reach out to find Peter, to pull him to the surface. The sun is already setting, the jagged fire fading. In the growing dark I can see his sinking face, down past where my feet kick. I heave in a breath and follow. There is no more hunger, the undertow gone gravity. I wonder if I have grown gills, or whether my lungs have expanded so I can stay under so long. Below me the current sweeps him, an undertow turns him over in a somersault and I see his eyes are closed, and the killer whales glide in and nudge him into the space between them. When he doesn't move, they decide to take him with them, down into a darkness blacker than them.

My lungs stretch, push against my ribs, and my eyes bulge for breath. An orca below me—I think they've come back for me. But it nuzzles its great head up under my feet and noses me to the surface, where my mouth explodes open and the air fish-knifes in, cutting my chest.

The rain smatters fiercely across the flat water. I float,

waiting for clouds of blood and bubbles to come up from where the orcas have taken Peter, but nothing. And then nothing. He's in the octopuses' garden now, in the shade.

I can't see the village from here, can't see the bodies of the other kids writhing on the beach. I will tell them the river sucked us in, and threw us out to sea and the killer whales got him like the other two kids. I won't tell them that his eyes were closed before the whales.

I float on the water, rain beating against my bare face. I wonder if we will grow old now that the rains have come. The thirst has hollowed out gaps under my ribs, things the killer whales might explain if they could talk. I roll over, and with slow, strong kicks, I aim my body for shore to find the others, to tell them.

braille

All that summer, weight gathering around the careful wait
of desire, not knowing what to want as the heat pressed
in, blurring the sight lines, the careful gather then release
of tired tired tired, holding on to the already rather than
reaching out in this thick of it, even to the width, the
breadth of that boy's wide, wide back. Shelter looks good.

Decreasing measure of the tide erasing its line and
re-drawing it in surges until the water nudges our feet,
and we sit here on this short log that surely won't float.

The first date you told me about the sensation of rain
falling on your bare back as you swam lengths in the out-
door pool, and I told you about the sleepy pain with which
a surgeon opens your body.

Asked you what your favourite scar was and you told
me how as a boy you once rode alongside a barbed-wire
fence in the dark and ·   ·   ·   ·
the punctuation of scars all up your side now, like Braille
for the love lost. The first time holding someone in so long,
I read you carelessly, and my fingers forgot to look for those
pauses, those ellipses. Much later now, I want to read back,
be more careful, but we only had that once so it's all left
to my fumble-touch-sleep hankering.

You were gravity from the first, the way sinkholes open
in the streets while we sleep, pulling whole cars in. These

hollow pockets where we store empty until they fall in on themselves, stare us in the face all open-mouthed.

Back to not wanting to sleep, back to filling the day with pocket grit, waiting and hiding so I'll see the sinking when it comes.

If I hadn't lost you to fear, I would have lost you to the water, you, the boy who does laps like some people swallow. In the pool by the ocean (because you like the word *ocean*, one syllable undertow slipping into the next) wondering how to talk to someone already underwater.

Some whales beat the surface to communicate across large distances, but I don't want them to think I am drowning. I'm not. Just sitting in the shallow end, knowing—longing pulls you out into the ocean a little more each moment. And me pulled along by the leaving, wondering what you see out there, pretending I don't know.

the melancholy contortionist

Fall. Ben can't believe he's thought it.

Fall. But there it is.

The man and the woman in the centre ring under the big top, the man a still and hunkered Atlas, the woman his mirror inverted, they meet only at the shoulders, her feet reaching to touch the tent far above. She could slip so easily, only the pressure between them holding her there, sprouting from his shoulder blades. And though Ben is drawn up by this fraught balance, he also imagines the man dropping the woman. Vertigo fear and desire for the fall.

A worse thing, far worse, if he'd wished this plummet on the acrobats or the tightrope walker. The woman contortionist is only five feet from the stage, less than a breath's distance. They fold together, a tight ligature of limbs from which her feet pierce and rise again for the peak of the circus tent, the scant spiderweb of cables taut and waiting for the acrobat's opposable feet. She emerges from him upside down, rigid, the crown of her head held in his right hand, the rest of her vertical, sprung, further now to fall as the man lifts his arm and her above his head. If she were to slip, she could break her neck. Ben never should have wished such a thing. Maybe it was envy. He does wish it might be him, held in those grave hands, balance and catastrophe.

The two of them do not smile, give no expression of effort or anticipation, their bodies shape new signs, mouth taut, architectural phrases. All that's left for the third-row lover are these hands he sits on as they strain to be set free. He sits not wanted, just wanting. Not watched. Watching.

Ben decides he must meet the male contortionist, if only to find out. What would be the first words out of his silence? It is a risk. Maybe the contortionist doesn't speak English. Maybe he speaks it too much, makes up for his stage silence by filling rooms with words like dizzy birds. Regardless, it is the last show of the last night in this city and Ben feels slippery.

— — —

A windy night and all the prickly seeds fall, crack open secrets of horse chestnuts smooth like the word *bolus* in a mouth. Ben stands by the back door well after the rain, and he wonders, do circus folk have groupies? He hunches his shoulders up in the cold with a shiver, watching the stage door for an exit.

What will be the first word from Ben's mouth when faced with the contortionist? He remembers the funeral mask of the contortionist's white face in the stage lights, feels suddenly foolish. Remembers when he was nineteen in the gallery in Athens, the wing of discarded marble statues, crowded in, little Greek widows worrying beads in rooms nearby, oblivious, how he leaned in close, his breath on the marble, the closest he'd been to a man yet, though that man was made of milk-white stone. Gods in the storeroom. There are no words. What can he say to escape the third row, the careful syntax of faces in a line, smiling, now sad, then laughing? Maybe he'll ask a question, any question so long as it asks, Did you see me there, there in the third row, wanting my shoulders pressed against yours, feet skyward, carried and lifted?

The door squeaks opens then, a pale light falling out into the street. The tumblers tumble out into the rain, roll down the street and away, talking in round sentences, the night washing into the spaces open for a moment, the door squeaking closed behind them. Once more waiting, waiting to be opened.

Then it opens, not suddenly but with purpose, like the contortionist knew just how the door wanted to be opened so it wouldn't squeak at all.

Ben imagined all he could, what he would say when the door burst open, what he would say as the contortionist stepped out under the awning.

Yet nothing on his tongue materializes as he stares open-mouthed at the contortionist, the woman stepping out behind him. They might be married, or lovers—Ben sees he has made a mistake. Can he say something that will keep the two contortionists from blending together, fading into each other's arms, folding up, saffron crocuses in swilling dark? Say something. Say something before they walk away.

"You were …" Ben tries.

"You're drenched," the contortionist says, and opens an umbrella. Ben had forgotten the rain running down his collar until the umbrella was above him, the rain pattering off its taut skin.

She says goodnight with a smile, half smirk. Is it a smile that's seen men wait here before? Ben worries the way only a circus groupie at a back door in the rain ought to.

The taut man in repose. Months later now. Ben thought it would be different than this, the rare glimpse of the lines going slack. But, he discovers instead, bodies made of such muscle never rest, push and pull even asleep. The contortionist twitches, having dog dreams in the dark of the room, murmurs, mumbling body and mouth releasing all they cannot say under the careful control of the stage lights, in the calculated circumference of the circus ring.

Ben thinks of staying awake all night, mapping the twitches and the murmurs on a graph line like dolphin sounds, imagining some quiet Rosetta Stone behind this strange vocabulary. He thinks, in moments, that he wants to kiss the contortionist, bring him awake a little, step out of the third row. Because he might be able to, especially if the contortionist kisses back. Why can't the watched and the watchers trade places? Why isn't he the one who is sleeping, half waking to a contortionist's quiet kiss? This longing is a known secret, something they both understand as simple as the placement of the salt and pepper shakers on the Arborite table by the window. Can't be that much of a crime, that terrible if the two of them are still here. If only he could sleep.

— — —

An unremarkable night, except that it's the last one in this city, the jagged glass buildings and the insistent ocean. On stage, they move and counter-move, each twitch of muscle a response. She moves too quickly tonight, ready to get in taxis, on airplanes, and shed the suitcase. He keeps her pace, gives her that.

He undresses, sheds the sweat-soaked tights, washes off in the sink what makeup he can, white still persisting behind his ears, the nape of his neck. There's always white left.

She waits for him in the hallway, pushes off the wall when she sees him. She has white makeup around her temples, a little Frankenstein's bride. He smiles.

They push through the stage door into the alley, wet gusts into them, makes him stumble on the step. He's spent all night maintaining their balance, has little equilibrium left. And then there, this lank man, the Modigliani mouth and sad slant of eyes, mumbles at him, steps, then trips into him, pulls the contortionist out from under the canopy.

Rain peppers the contortionist's shaved head, staccato fingers thrumming his attention so he tilts his head back to see what the rain wants. That Modigliani mouth on his, a flash of warm in the deluge, a bottom lip answer he doesn't remember asking for.

The contortionist breaks the kiss. The man's eyes remind him of blue marbles he had when he was six, but the contortionist turns to make sure she is gone.

It's not that she might be jealous. They aren't romantically involved, but there are moments in the day or sometimes at night when he knows where she'll be, the way he anticipates, knows each twitch of the muscles on her forearms, knows her left shoulder is weak and she will tense her right in fear of it, and knows how to move them both past that to the next posture. Fluid.

Except the once. She'd fallen in love once. It was September and they were putting on a show to start the season before they went on tour. She'd been gone for days, missed rehearsal, and he'd been unable to reach her by phone. When she did finally show up, her shoulders were tensed forward, her head listing to the right. She was distracted, and she wouldn't look at him. A simple planche. A posture that was the first letter of their language, and she leaned back from him, not gradually trusting her feet under his armpits, but jerked into posture without any attention. He cleared his throat. They don't make sounds. Not usually, but she was moving with disregard.

They pulled each other up, face to face. He looked at her with as much exclamation as he could, but her eyes were opaque, drowned. He lifted her up then, she stepped onto his shoulders. Then stepped onto his hands, stood high above him. She was to backbend over, place her hands where her feet were, but she flung herself with too much abandon, and his arms shook with the shift in balance so she fell over his back. Quick, he sprang around and caught her, saved her from falling Icarus into the stage floor.

The audience applauded in an uproar, thinking this was her dismount.

"What?" he whispered at her angrily. She flushed a little around her neck and clavicles—a blush from a woman who never blushed—stone overflowing.

She inhaled, clasped his left forearm with hers, beginning still without looking at him. They lowered down and back, planche again, this time with him extending from her, a habitual finale, the audience amazed her small legs and feet could hold the two of them stretched out, held in perfect balance, lateral, one long horizon. Her breathing was rapid, though, more rapid than usual as they contorted, unfurled as he leaned back musculature and ribs, unfeeling.

Just the once. The contortionist in the rain turns back, sees the man has pulled away, has sunk chin to chest but then looks back up, a sweetness in the pleading look. The contortionist bites his bottom lip, still tasting that Modigliani pulpy mouth.

— — —

She knows his body, too, knows the thickened scar tissue mid back where he tore the muscles one spring, how his legs are prone to shake if he's not had enough water or vitamin C, the left knee tendons and muscles, fabric already fraying, ready to tear. So she must forget, a sort of faith so she can trust the hands that hold her, lift her, balance her precariously above the stage floor, grace something she gives herself twice a day. Three times on Saturdays.

— — —

She's gone and Ben stands a mere foot from the contortionist who kissed him. He feels he must say something. "Would you ... would you like to go for coffee?"

"I don't drink coffee."

"Then ... juice?"

"I thought we'd just go back to my place."

Ben nods. Even though he's afraid it's too easy. He's been raised to believe easy come easy go, some strange moral to look for difficult loves, as though hard to get means hard to lose. So halfway back to the hotel he asks the contortionist if they can go down to the water first.

The gesture, the contortionist points out later, of a man trying to turn sex into a date. Ben doesn't disagree, only blushes and lowers his head.

They walk to the beach, along line of sand hissing in the rain, hushed lap of the waves. Ben turns to the contortionist, mouth stumbling, seeking some way to say he wants to go already, wants to be in a room, in a hotel, high above the water, wrung tight and twisted. Contorted. He wants to appear unobtainable enough to make the contortionist want him back, but he also just wants to be obtained. Fighting difficult with easy, waiting for the now of a kiss. The contortionist interrupts him with his lips.

A frustrating montage of taxi, sidewalk, lobby, elevator, lurid hallway, door, hotel room, then a tearing, tumbling, stumble, and fall. Violence in the luge from general to particular.

The sex isn't spectacular so much as it isn't very good at all. They are too tired so sleep eventually takes priority. Can't bode well, Ben thinks. But, he had wanted difficult to win over easy.

— — —

The contortionist remembers their first kiss, out there in the rain. Clearly enough. But dancers and performers kiss for everything, hello, goodbye. He remembers more what came next. How the man dripping rain stepped back into the streetlight and the rain, a stab-wound look. The contortionist wanted to keep looking into that face, its white bare clarity, the sweet juice-box stain spreading across his face. But then this long bracket of a man stepped back, pulled the contortionist into his arms, crushing them together, cheek to jugular.

In the embrace, the contortionist felt this stranger's breathing, his heart a sparrow in a wicker cage. He almost laughed then, imagining how he could hold this frightened creature in his cupped palms, but then the stranger grasped him closer and suddenly the contortionist's mind fogged. The open palms held the contortionist, not this man with the Modigliani mouth and the persistent rain.

Through the fog he tried to remember the last time someone held him like this, a tight fist that says take this instead of give me. The contortionist stopped breathing for fear that the inhale of his rising ribcage might push the man away. Then he grabbed back, from foot to face pressing into him, rigidly, to hold, to take.

— — —

Early morning, Ben watches him roll his shirts, his pants, tucking them into a small rolly suitcase. The contortionist is leaving again, another tour. Ben rides the Metro with him to the studio where the bus waits for the performers. He sees her there, realizes he has to say goodbye beside a bus with her watching, and thinks she must be wondering why the graceful fall in love with the clumsy. She knows this with her half smile, the way her eyes watch traffic or passersby across the street, looking stage right and away like she's never once imagined he has ever left the audience.

Ben imagines she loves that way, too, each lover just an audience. Then shakes his head, for fear the two contortionists might share this spectacle habit. Maybe, though, Ben hopes, just maybe his contortionist is different, has a desire to tumble off the stage, fall free of each look and pose.

Standing outside the bus, the luggage loaded, Ben searches the contortionist's eyes for this longing. The contortionist hugs him, pats him on the back the way men do to bracket feelings. As he climbs the steps of the bus, Ben turns and rushes to the Metro entrance and down the escalator, leaving before the bus can pull away and leave him first.

Back at their apartment, Ben strips naked and blankets the bed with his limbs, glum. He inhales the nape scent left on the contortionist's pillow, remembers long muscles running down sides, thick trunks of legs, two dimples in small of back, a small catalogue searching for proof of the contortionist. Afternoon light, bare of dust motes, hankers in the cut of the window blinds.

— — —

Contortionists are well written, Ben thinks. Each muscle succinct. A body written not as a question, but as an answer. Such thoughts addle him as he watches the two perform

again, the fourth time in three weeks. Not that he's bored.
No. He's provoked. Each and every time, there in the third
row, provoked. Provoked and jealous, envious she gets the
taut, unshakeable illusion of stone.

Seeing the contortionist's body rigid and wrought there
on the stage, he is provoked, too, into wondering if he
knows that body at all. At home, under sullen shadows,
he sometimes slackens the sheets, traces rivers of pulse
and muscle down the length of the contortionist, fearful
almost. A body in repose but so often in pain. Nights after
performances, Ben watches the lights of passing cars splay
across the ceiling of the bedroom, weight of time, and
his wary vigil, the contortionist's body twitching to some
unreachable rhythm out beyond the shutters, the treetops,
the streetlights. He sometimes puts his fingertips or his
lips there gently, mid back a little thicker with scar tissue,
the muscles clenching, and sometimes the twitching
stops. Calmed. Heard. And he thinks to himself, we can't
touch ourselves this way. And we wonder where loneliness
comes from.

A Saturday show, Ben realizes he no longer wants to
be a contortionist. He's been imagining he would wake up
and have the balance and musculature to lift that woman
up into the air with just his right hand cupping the crown
of her head, the same way he would, as a child, jump from
ledges once a year waiting for his superhero powers to come.

"Cheap grace," he'd heard a woman in the elevator at
work say to a temp. The phrase has been clattering around
in his head trying to collect sense. Somewhere between the
twelfth and the fourteenth floor he wondered if there were
any other kinds.

— — —

Ben meets the contortionist backstage after the show. He doesn't go into the dressing room, even though the contortionist told him to. He waits in the hall, pretending to be interested in the walkways above, the cables, lights hanging in the dark. Waiting. He doesn't hear voices or sounds from inside. He thinks maybe he missed him, maybe he's left already.

Then the door next to the men's opens and it's her. She gives him the smallest of nods.

"Great show," Ben says, and she nods again, pulls her trench coat around her, cinching the waist as she walks down the hall and away without saying goodbye.

The men's dressing room door opens, the tumblers tumbling out first again, off to find an all-night liquor store, and then Ben can see the contortionist there, sitting, leaning forward trying to do up his shoes. He hangs in the door watching, sees the contortionist's broad back arched over, his hands struggling with the laces. Ben's seen this before, how after a show the contortionist becomes senseless and clumsy. He kneels down in front of the contortionist, puts his folded program on the concrete floor, and takes the laces from him. The contortionist looks up, gives Ben a wavering smile, then leans back in the chair, the exhausted Atlas, eyes closed. Ben first ties the left, then the right shoe, double bows. He stands, leans in with a hand on each of the contortionist's knees, and kisses his upturned face softly on each eye. Taking his hand, he pulls him to his feet, more a gesture than an effort, the contortionist's hand heavy in Ben's. Ben slings the contortionist's pack over his shoulder and pulls him to the door, wanting to get him home. They dodge the other performers leaving, the stage hands still cleaning up. Out the backstage door and into the rain.

There, under an umbrella, a mouth as pulpy as Ben's, stands a blonde boy, the circus program in his hand, face scarlet hope as he sees the contortionist, loses its shaky smile when he sees the contortionist's hand in Ben's.

The contortionist sees none of this, but walks past the blonde umbrella man, pulling Ben through the rain.

Ben shatters against the alley walls under the streetlight, pieces left dashed under an umbrella in the rain, unseen, some caught in the alley detritus remembering a kiss in another alley, and the last piece, his hand small and pale in the contortionist's insistent hand, pulled towards home.

— — —

He is the fluid ebbing measure of her balance, yet tonight she feels each gesture in response to her own, numb and metric, can feel the jerk of his muscles clenching, releasing too slowly, a rhythm she tries to unfurl, quicken with pulse. His grip on her forearms, cat's tongue and crushing, but she's glad as sweat pours off him tonight. Maybe he has a fever.

Between dos à dos and planche, a moment where their faces press side to side, as she pulls back, preparing to move into the reverse planche, she looks into his face, and though she usually blurs her eyes impressionistic, this time she sees he's looking back at her. Earnest even. A question. And then he looks off into the audience as they turn away from one another—she sees he looks towards the third row.

She places a foot on each of his knees, gently and subtly pinches the skin on his arm where she holds on, but he nudges his arm free of the pinch, grabs her wrist, cinches his hand around it, leans back so she does too, balancing him in planche, this long line, both their faces flung back, pleading to the canopy of the tent above. She won't forgive him for that.

She skips the applause, doesn't change, wraps her overcoat

around her and rushes out into the rain, to the line of cabs waiting for the audience. He should call her. He should explain.

— — —

The contortionist caught in slow turns of agony, the rolling, rolling pain, his mid back, the scar tissue torn again at the gym this morning, back extensions. And sometimes, he says, it feels good when the throbbing pushes, lifts, just right, not jagged.

Running his hands up and down the contortionist, lightly, Ben hopes to smooth the pain's ridges, but this pain leaves him outside.

"Please. Stop." Touch just another stimulus in a mind already unable to process it all. The contortionist's legs flexing, then rigid, breathing. What language is this? Ben wonders. How to respond? Three kisses on the right spot might lead to forgetfulness.

Even the contortionist's mother probably can't read this body now, though she's apparently well read, must be after nine children, he half of seven and eight—twins who look nothing alike.

Ben wonders if it might be true, that twins are more prone to relationships and have a sense of how two people can be close. Or might it instead be like being born married, lead to claustrophobia, or an inarticulate desire for travelling?

— — —

The third night, the third performance she's endured this constrained man beneath her, she has supported him, finding balance for them. Her muscles feel like they'll seize up and pull her into a ball all at once so she'll roll into the orchestra pit.

She's seen him in love before, seen the contortionist through the quickening, slight lunge to each posture, and then the slow constricting, the cinching cord. And this man, he shows up anyway. She knows just where Ben's sitting, in the same seat for three nights now. Imagines his blank face. We fight for wonder, she thinks to herself. Long for a chorus of gasps. Not this blank face. She wants to know why. She didn't see him as the persistent type. Why doesn't he just go home? She knows she can't take much more, isn't even angry anymore, but just tired now. She has licked her bottom lip raw, chewed the inside of her mouth. She is on the brink of saying something.

— — —

Saturday, Ben returns to the audience once more. Three nights now, and he thinks maybe tonight, feels close, like he might be able to fall back into the faceless deep end of the reverent crowd. Maybe he can forget the ragged body stretching on the living room floor, the painful sleep murmurs. But then he has to forget the smooth, round rise of the contortionist's ass in the mute Sunday morning light. The music crescendos and he sees only their two bodies, stretching for balance, stretching out, and for a moment, monumental. Then it's the crown of Ben's head cradled in the contortionist's thick hand, his feet in the rafters. Held yet flung, a caramel salt ambivalence. Ben bare white under the stage lights, folds in, brought down—

She slips. A shudder pulse, how buildings shake before collapsing to rubble. The contortionist twists to the right, both hands reaching in panic. Her body lurches, tries to tuck, pull the balance back. She falls. His hands grasp, manic, can't hold, swirling away from him, her head hits the stage first with the sound bodies make when they're hit by cars or blunt objects. The sound that resounds in an audience's memory, later, as they turn over and over trying to find sleep.

The contortionist brackets over her, searching her face.

That beholding, that reverence, Ben sees it clearly, the contortionist's left hand pressed against the side of her face.

When the house lights come up so the paramedics can gurney their way down to the stage, there is an empty seat in the third row. The audience, mouths covered, hush, all eyes caught by prone woman and the man leaning over her, the curtains torn down, the house lights up. Still they stand watching.

— — —

Or a Monday, counterfeit last leaves, wary witness of racoons, the lagoon where they sit and the park bench, an audience of two. They place words in the air, take them down and feed them to wandering ducks. The contortionist has Sundays and Mondays off, but he spent Sunday at the gym, off on his own, an umbrella and the Peruvian sweater he got on tour years ago. He wanders the city and Ben waits, knowing the words will come and knowing there's no prying them loose before then.

Ben imagines all the things that might be preoccupying the contortionist: infidelity, boredom, or worse, nothing. He places each one in his mouth, worries it around with his tongue, then takes it out and places it on the coffee table, picking up the next or the last.

Then Monday, the contortionist calls from the living room, suggests a walk.

An ending in increments, the grave and glacial. Brittle shards and glue-stuck fingers. The lagoon, mere blocks to the apartment when the end finally comes. Ben marvels at the convenience.

He's been having sex with one of the tumblers, the one with the faux-hawk and the slack jaw.

Ben can't cry. Can't breathe. It seems like the right thing, perfect casting. He nods as the contortionist explains, how it happened, the stress of touring, someone bought a box of wine, the contortionist wondered how it would feel to have an affair, something like that. But Ben is dividing up belongings in his head, the CDs, how the contortionist won't want the kitchen stuff as left to his own devices he eats only instant noodles and vitamins. How Ben will ask the contortionist to leave. How he has the right to ask this. An ending with justice and clarity. Ben can handle that.

— — —

But, instead, a Friday night. Ben doesn't go to the performance. An evening of unremarkable things, a book on topiary, going to the kitchen and looking at the dishes but then leaving them for the topiary, flipping. A thought to clean the bathroom, but he decides that's a morning task. He stands at the bedroom window looking past the streetlights and insists he won't think about the two of them, across town, bathed in stage light, face to face in metamorphosis. Television, sundry channels, he nods off on the couch, a dream about gardens, rain, running.

The lock clicking open, *swish* then *cachunk* of the door opening and closing. Ben turns over on the couch and his book thunks to the floor. No one calls out from the hall. He sits up, face in hands, scrunches sleep away. Picks up his empty teacup and pads from the living room to the hall, this scene laid out before him: black rain jacket, a sodden shoe beached on its side, jeans like shed snakeskin, another shoe, upright, deflated T-shirt, a line of debris running from the front door to the bedroom. He follows the evidence until he stands in the bedroom doorway, sees the contortionist's impact, limbs scattered, naked, flung. Wants to follow, wonders what might come next, yet stands there in the door, trying to imagine.

acknowledgements

I want to first and foremost thank the friends and family who supported me through the writing, particularly my aunt/sister Donna, my two amazing grandmothers, and my dad. I come from a long line of storytellers and feel honoured to add my voice to theirs.

Particular love and thanks to Rachel, Susan, Rhys, and Theo, for the place they call home and lovingly share with me. Also thanks to those friends and family who have shared their homes to this itinerant writer: Tom Fedechko, Mark Anthony Jarman, Daphne and Bill, and the Wrigleys.

Adoration and thanks to Kaleena Kiff and Allison Mack, the two women who listen to my stories and tell me theirs, with whom I share a brainheartsoul. And to the waterboys, the tall-tale tellers, my other brothers, Mark, Lucas, and Morris.

My cherished and lovely readers: Russell Westhaver, Ruth Dyckfehderau, and Susan Goldberg. And the two biggest cheerleaders I know, Ward Bingham and Sarah Gray. And all my other cheer squad, John, Kristen K., Sheila, Jones, Monica, Judith, Bronwen, Mark C., Tamara, Day, Dionne, and Adam.

Gratitude to the Nocion Café in Quito, Ecuador, where final rewrites were done in the shadow of a volcano while sipping Ecuador's best espresso surrounded by the most supportive people. And thanks to Christopher Smith, my intrepid travel buddy.

Immense and vast thanks to Suzette Mayr, Tiffany Foster, Natalie Olsen, Douglas Barbour, Lou Morin, and Andrew Sharp at NeWest Press. And to Nathalie Daoust for the amazing cover photo.

This book was written with support from the Ontario Arts Council, the Alberta Foundation for the Arts, the Canada Council for the Arts, the Banff Centre for the Arts, and the Sage Hill Writer's Retreat.

Some of the stories in this collection have been previously published in the following publications:

"Wabi Sabi" in *Wascana Review* 40, 1 & 2
(Spring and Fall 2005).

"Braille" published as "All That Summer"
and "Waves" in *Quickies* 3.

"Sunflowers" in *Grain Magazine*, 28.3
(Winter 2001), 9–16.

"Undertow" in *Other Voices* (Summer 2000).

"Freighters" in *Quickies* 2, Arsenal Pulp Press
(1999).

"Sweet Tooth" published as "Passion and Cold
Soup" in *Event Magazine*, 25.3 (December 1996).

R.W. Gray was born and raised on the northwest coast of British Columbia, and received a PhD in Poetry and Psychoanalysis from the University of Alberta in 2003. He is the author of two serialized novels in *Xtra West* magazine (*Waterboys* and *Tide Pool Sketches*) and has published poetry in various journals and anthologies, including *Arc*, *Grain*, *Event*, and *dANDelion*. He has also had ten short screenplays produced. He currently teaches Film at the University of New Brunswick in Fredericton. *Crisp* is his first book.